Dancing Girl
of the
Indus Valley

Dancing Girl of the Indus Valley

Arshud Mahmood

illustrated by AliA

Edited by Martha Fuller
Layout and design by Sharon E Rawlins
Artwork by AliA

INDUS WEST
induswest22@gmail.com
Tustin, California

ISBN (Print) #979-8-9870810-0-6
ISBN (eBook) #979-8-9870810-1-3

Printed in the United States of America

To my late wife,
Maliha Mendoza Mahmood
who inspired, encouraged and supported me
in every activity and venture— including
the start of this book.
Sadly she did not live to see its completion.

CONTENTS

Prologue

Four thousand, five hundred (4,500) years ago there were three civilizations in the world: Egypt along the River Nile, Mesopotamia in the valley of the Tigris and Euphrates rivers, and the Indus Valley along the River Indus and its five tributaries. Egypt and Mesopotamia were empires ruled by Pharaohs and Kings, but cooperative Town Councils governed the Indus Valley communities. Egypt and Mesopotamia left extensive written records, but the Indus Valley left none.

This story is set in the Indus Valley 4,500 years ago.

First three civilizations, c.2,500 B.C.—Egypt, Mesopotamia, and Indus Valley inlcuding Harappa.

CHAPTER 1

The Spring Dance

Spring came early this year to the Indus Valley, throwing the residents of the town of Harappa into a frenzy of activity in preparation for The Spring Festival. The festival will take place over three days —with the first day reserved for private ceremonies of ablutions and prayers at home, as well as setting up the main festival site in the middle of the town square. The food stalls are being stocked up and the seating areas under the trees cleaned. The site for the Spring Dance, the most festive and jubilant event of the whole festival, is cleared of even the smallest pebbles and smeared with a thin layer of fine clay mud to protect the dancers' feet. On the morning of the dance contest, water is sprayed onto the dance floor and seating area to keep the temperature cool. Just before the contest begins, rose water is sprinkled in the performance area to freshen the air. The scent of damp earth and the fragrance of rose water are subtle but effective in elevating the spectators' mood and energizing the dancers for what is to come.

The five-man Town Council, or the *Panchayat*, has been overseeing the preparations. The head of the council welcomes the residents. "We thank the Goddess for blessing our town and our festivities. Over the last three days you have done your devotions, eaten good food, seen acrobats, jugglers, magicians, clowns, and wrestlers. You may also have competed in skill games with your friends and neighbors." There are muffled cheers as people look up in appreciation. The council head raises one hand and the crowd quiets. "Now we present our main event—the dance contest. Welcome again. Enjoy the performance."

The troupes of dancers composed of young men and women have prepared and rehearsed for days—separately for men and women. It is a dance-off between the male and female troupes. A friendly but fierce competition. The pivotal moves and songs have been kept secret from the other side.

The dance begins and cheers go up each time the girls swirl gracefully, or the boys display their athleticism. The male and female troupes dance alternately. Each successive routine builds in tempo and complexity. The young men are clearly winning, in large part due to the lead dancer Ramey of the jewelry makers' clan. His athleticism and leadership of the troupe are vital as he gives hints and signals to the dancers when crucial moves and steps are to be executed. The men dance their finale and leave the main performing area. The young women come into the center with intricate steps to match the fast tempo of the men. The lead girl is a skilled but frail beauty from the weavers' clan. In the middle of the routine, when the lead girl is lifting, dropping and turning her feet, she gives a short, painful cry and falls to the ground. She has twisted her ankle. The dance stops and she is helped away from the area. There are hushed questions.

"What is to be done now?"

"Is it over?"

"What about their finale?"

"Have the boys won?"

The dancers glance at each other, while the spectators wait anxiously, looking around. Everyone is hungry and the crowd is getting restless. The girls wait to see who will go up and take the place at the front to match up with the boys' performance.

There is a brisk movement in the back of the girls' troupe as one girl steps forward to take the lead position at the front. Most people do not know who she is. She wears a rose in her hair that she plucks out as she stands in a provocative pose waiting for the music to begin. Dressed in red block print clothes made of thin cotton with a bead necklace, her left arm is covered with bangles from her wrist to her shoulder. On her other arm she wears four wide bangles. Holding the rose, she gestures as if beckoning the spectators to watch and issuing a challenge to the boys. She holds this pose for several moments to let the audience take it all in, then jangles her right arm, signaling the musicians to resume.

The music starts up again with the musicians accelerating the tempo from where they left off and the dance troupe comes to life. The lead girl's skill and physicality infuse the energy and verve that has been missing. The change is so dramatic that even the most tired and hungry spectators take notice. The new girl's shapely body and intriguing features add to her mystique. She seems to have picked up the moves during the early part of the routine—her grace and beauty make up for the rest. As the dancers heat up and begin to sweat, they are repeatedly sprinkled with rose water. The new girl dazzles the crowd and the dance ends with loud applause. Clearly the girls have won. The other girls in the troupe come up to her with smiles and hugs to express their sheer joy and gratitude in leading them to victory.

Ramey, the lead young man cannot take his eyes off the new dancing girl. Even from a distance, he feels a strange ethereal attraction towards her. He senses her discomfort at the sudden attention from the crowd and walks over to her. She is drenched in

Ramey

a mixture of perspiration and rose water—the thin cotton clothing clings to her body. Whatever of her form is not obvious, Ramey's imagination fills in. The blended scent arouses a primal feeling in him as if he has always known and loved her.

"I am Ramey," he says.

She meets his gaze briefly and lowers her eyes as if to examine her toenails dyed red by crushing red oleander petals. A faint smile comes to her lips and her eyebrows arch up. Keeping her head lowered, she gives him a sideways glance—amused. This arch look of hers pulls at Ramey's heart.

"I know who you are," she says under her breath, still contemplating her toenails.

He struggles to find his voice and clears his throat. "But I know not who you are?"

"Zara," she says softly, "I am Zara."

"Zara," he says slowly, as if tasting her name. "You live in Harappa?"

She gestures in the affirmative.

"How is it that I have not seen you before?"

She looks up and meets his gaze for a moment. "But I have seen you." She takes a deep breath. "We live on the north side."

This town is getting big, he thinks, but is left on his own to guess which family she is from. He knows the jewelry makers all live on the south side.

Zara

"Are you hungry Zara? Would you like some food?"

With a steady gaze, she looks approvingly at him. It has been a long walk this morning, and then the spirited dance finale. She is famished.

"Just wait here," Ramey says. He walks briskly toward the food stalls and jostles his way through the crowd. He returns with two clay bowls filled with a mix of lentils and vegetables, emitting a light fragrance of seasoning, and two wooden spoons. In his other hand he balances two clay goblets of a cool and refreshing yogurt drink. They sit down under the shade of a nearby tree. He feels the same strange attraction to her that transcends any physical appeal, though he cannot ignore her beauty. He has always been thought of as a person who only likes one person—himself—so this attraction towards another is new to him.

After eating, they talk about the festival, the dance, the weather, and everything else but themselves. Before long, they know each other's opinions on many things, without saying what they think of each other. Finally, Ramey asks a couple of direct questions and finds out she is from one of the cloth-weaving families.

A couple of weeks later, he walks up to the north side of town, and after two stops at the wrong houses and a few enquiries, he finds her house. Zara's father, Dogar, meets him politely and Ramey is able to chat with Zara for a while. His visits continue through the summer, and he gets to know her family well. Dogar is on the trading side of business, rather than weaving, while Zara is artistic and helps her father select rare colors and patterns that serendipitously predict the coming year's favorites. Various weaving families in the community prepare bolts of cloth according to Zara's designs, and Dogar travels far and wide selling them. While Ramey never quite understands the weaving intricacies of warp and weft, he can comfortably discuss the nuances of buying and selling. Dogar knows nothing about jewelry making, but becomes fond of the young man who knows about marketing

By the end of summer, Ramey senses that Zara likes him, and with the good response from her father, he feels brave enough to think he and Zara will one day be married. His family has begun to wonder why he spends so much time with the cloth weaving community, to the point of neglecting his own jewelry making chores. He decides to bring it up with his mother.

"Mother, I want you to meet a girl."

"Is that the *Dancing Girl*?" she asks.

"*Dancing Girl*?"

"Yes, what is her name—Tara, Zara?

"It's Zara. What have you heard about her?"

"Just that people have not forgotten her since the Spring Festival, and it is now nearly fall."

"Well, yes, it is the same girl, Zara."

"Zara is an odd name."

"Well, that is the name her parents gave her."

"A cloth weaver's daughter? Your uncle's daughters are pretty. And your aunt's daughters are very obedient. And what about the daughters of our neighbor? They are very hard working."

"Mother," he says in a calm but firm tone, "I have been playing with them since we were small. They are like my own sisters."

"But this Zara is not one of us."

"One of *us*?"

"Not from a jewelry making family," she treads lightly.

"And?" Ramey is not going to let it go easily.

"But a cloth trader's daughter."

"And?"

Ramey's mother is losing her patience.

"The weavers work with cotton."

"And potters work with clay and farmers grow crops."

He understands very well that his mother is reminding him Zara is not from the top rung of the social ladder—not from a jewelry making family. Cloth weavers were below them, so why would he want to step down.

A similar conversation is repeated a couple of times between Ramey and his mother. Finally, she decides to take a different approach.

"And what will your uncle Banzil say? He has been so secretive even our cousins don't know about it."

Ramey does not have to be told what she is talking about. Even all the family members have not been told. Ramey knows that his Uncle Banzil who has been the head of the family since his father died, is very particular about guarding the knowledge and does not want the information to seep out. Ramey has not resolved in his mind how to handle it with Zara, but he wants her and wants her soon. He knows girls that become well known in the community are married off early—and she has indeed become well known.

Ramey's mother finally relents and agrees to meet Zara. This is essentially an interview, but at least it signals some measure of acceptance into the family. Ramey is worried about several relatives meeting Zara all at once and making her nervous.

"You will be alone when you meet her, is that right?"

His mother promises she will be alone. She offers to walk to Zara's house to meet her, but her knees have been giving her problems again, and although Ramey appreciates the sentiment, he does not think it is practical for her to make the long walk. The day is set. Ramey goes to Zara's house and brings her back to meet his mother. Dressed in modest beige cotton clothes, Zara does not look anything like the vivacious dancing girl from the Spring Dance.

As Ramey and Zara enter their neighborhood, a boy who has been sitting under a tree takes one look at them and runs toward his house like a herald. As they get closer, Ramey senses people peeking out from half-open doors, ready to spring into action and join his mother. He realizes his mother might be alone in their house now, but she would soon be surrounded by a host of relatives and neighbors, all eager to meet Zara. She is going to end up facing a whole crowd of uncles, aunts, cousins and other relatives—they are all going to be there. As they near the house, his heart sinks. He can sense the anticipation building in the neighborhood and begins to lose his nerve.

Not only does Ramey know, but Zara has guessed it won't be just his mother and that all the relatives will show up—some to welcome her, others out of curiosity, and some to criticize her. Ramey is nervous but senses Zara's anxiety is greater than his. As they come within sight of their house, his throat is dry and his stomach churns. The shadow of the tall *shisham* tree in front of the house is nearing their front door, indicating the exact hour at which his mother will be expecting them.

He cannot go through with this. He feels like bolting, leaving Zara there, and abandoning the whole enterprise of this marriage and his chosen girl. And that is almost what he does. He invents a phony excuse and points out the door to her.

"That is my house," he says.

"We are going in, right?" she asks, expecting him to say yes. Perhaps hold her hand and walk in side by side.

He shakes his head, "No, you are going in."

"And you?"

"I have to go and check on the new drill for beads."

She looks at his face with disappointment and dismay. Is this the man I am supposed to spend my life with? Is this the person I am expecting to protect me through thick and thin? A dark shadow passes across her face. It lasts only a moment. Slowly, her expression changes to a steely resolve. If this man doesn't have the spine, then I'll have to be the strong one.

Within sight of the house, he bolts. Like a gutless coward, he leaves her by herself to meet his mother and later face all his relatives. Zara pushes the door open and enters Ramey's house. A well-dressed middle-aged woman stands in the center of the courtyard smiling. This must be Ramey's mother, Zara decides. She approaches gracefully and bends down to touch her feet. The woman catches her arms on the way down, preventing Zara from performing this ritual—and embraces her.

"So, you are the girl my son is enchanted with."

"And you are the woman who raised such a wonderful man," Zara says.

She kisses his mother on her right and left cheeks and holds both her hands. A strong aroma of flavorful cooking from inside the house reaches Zara, and she tries to hide her smile. This is no ordinary daily meal for just this household—it is a feast for a large group. Her guess is confirmed—a large number of guests are expected.

Ramey's mother leads Zara to a comfortable seating area under the shade of an overhang roof. They are still holding hands and exchanging pleasantries as relatives trickle in. Ramey's mother tries to introduce her, but Zara is quicker in getting up, hugging the younger ones and trying to touch the feet of the older ones. The relatives must have agreed on the order in which they were going to arrive because by the end of the hour, the courtyard is filled with extended family and nearby neighbors, all eager to meet Zara. She is up to the task, full of smiles, pleasantries, and expressions of respect and friendship towards everyone.

Two hours later in the afternoon, Ramey finally shows up. Zara has managed to charm his mother

The Spring Dancers

and everyone else. She never mentions his lapse of courage and courtesy, nor does his mother. But he never forgets it. There are many things in his life he may come to regret and occasions when he may not act or may act foolishly. But this will remain a blot on his conscience and probably his most cowardly act.

Zara's lively personality and her open-minded and welcoming nature prove to be a blessing. She quickly blends into Ramey's immediate family, and soon thereafter, into the bead making clan. Two months pass when his mother wants to know when they will get married, but Ramey still has not resolved his Uncle Banzil's secret project—or how to introduce Zara into his secret.

CHAPTER 2

Dreams of the Outworld

Uncle Banzil's secret project began almost two years ago. More and more people have been offering the soapstone steatite beads at lower and lower prices and the family wants to move up to a higher tier of jewelry making. The strategy Uncle Banzil devises is to create a masterpiece bead of unprecedented length from a rare gemstone. He searches the northern mountains and returns with a gold-streaked, deep blue lapis lazuli—the stone from heaven, used along with gold for important items such as the funeral masks of Egyptian pharaohs including Tutankhamen. Its brilliant blue color is considered a reflection of the sky, and when found with gold streaks is the ultimate gem of the Bronze Age. What gives lapis lazuli its lasting charm is its hardness, but this very quality is a hindrance to bead making—a bronze drill is too soft.

Uncle Banzil scours the eastern desert and finds carborundum, an unattractive black mineral harder than lapis lazuli. When black carborundum powder is poured around a bronze drill, it will grind through lapis lazuli, to make beads as long as 7 centimeters. Uncle's goal is to make these long gold-streaked, deep blue beads and market them in Mesopotamia. He plans to take Ramey along to initiate him in selling in the Outworld beyond the Indus Valley.

Lapis Lazuli

Ramey has been told by Uncle about the river valley to the west—a great empire with unparalleled riches. The social structure of such a society is beyond Ramey's comprehension. He has heard of kings, palaces, temples and priests but these words do not convey clear images to him. The palaces in the empire are rumored to be full of unique and expensive artifacts. Perhaps one of these palaces might have need for unique jewelry such as the long lapis beads and other gemstones of impeccable quality. And what about the priests who control the temples? They might have the resources to acquire some of the jewelry. In any case, it means a long voyage to the west. All this is swirling in Ramey's head, but he is not worried—Uncle Banzil will be with him and explain everything. Ramey carries on his romance with Zara and they begin discussing a date for their wedding. The only hindrance is that Uncle Banzil wants Ramey to travel with him to Sumer before getting married. He fears Ramey will become busy with domestic affairs and reluctant to travel.

Ramey's first task is to tell Zara about the secret super gems. He goes through the description although she is not sure why it has to be a secret. He must also convince her this separation is necessary.

One day when they are alone, he clears his throat—a gesture that alarms her—she knows there is nothing stuck in his throat, except his own emotions.

"Zara."

She looks straight into his eyes, which unnerves Ramey.

"I have to go away for a while."

"Will you be back in two days? My sister is coming to visit."

"No," he says, "it will be longer. Probably a month."

She has spoken with young women in the jewelry community. All those married to traders like Ramey have endured separations, though none that last beyond a couple of weeks. Zara understands the need for the trip but doesn't accept it as fair treatment toward her. Why can't he sell his jewelry to the nearby towns and communities? Why does it have to be Ramey? Why can't one of his cousins go for the trading trip?

"If I take my jewelry far, it will fetch a higher price. I'll bring you back a woolen shawl."

This is a cheap trick. He knows she enjoys touching a beautiful shawl. There are only a few woolen ones in Harappa, mostly in dull colors. She would love a shawl dyed a brilliant red and would carry it everywhere on a chilly day. Some people would think she is showing off, but she would not care. Many people in town are already jealous of her.

Zara is still unwilling to accept Ramey's travels even as a tradition of the jewelers. But she understands the greater affluence and social status being married into a jewelry making family will afford her. All her childhood friends and cousins will look up to her with admiration and envy.

She takes a new tack, "Why does it have to be you?"

"I can convince people easily," he offers, "my cousins cannot."

She looks at him suspiciously. "Is that how you won me over so quickly? I know you are clever," she says, her face conveying affection, but there is a glint in her eye as she looks askance at him. Her eyebrow arches up while a smile breaks out on her lips. Whenever she begins expressing admiration for him, Ramey is never sure if she is being serious or teasing him. But he likes this arch look of hers. He grabs her hand, pulls her over, and hugs her tight. She melts in his arms, clinging to him like a vine around an oak tree.

A son is born to one of Ramey's cousins after many years of marriage. The newborn's parents decide to hold a celebration in an inner courtyard.

The whole jewelry making community is invited. Before the feast, a program of festivities has been planned, including a juggler and a clown to entertain the children. Several of the family members had missed the Spring Dance but heard of Zara's performance. They ask Zara if she would repeat her dance for them. She is reluctant, but when Ramey's mother asks her, she decides to oblige. Without her troupe of female dancers and without the male dance troupe, the atmosphere and mood of the Spring Dance will be impossible to recreate—but she promises to do her best.

News of her repeat performance spreads throughout the neighborhood. When she arrives, the courtyard is overflowing with people. She is intimidated and wants to change her mind, but the young cousins beg her and promise to do anything she wants. She hesitantly walks to the center of the gathering. The musicians who provided accompaniment at the Spring Dance have been engaged, so she will be able to relive some of the dramatic mood of that occasion.

As she begins her movements, the musicians rapidly bring it to the crescendo, and then hold it at that intensity for an extended period—far longer than at the Spring Dance. Zara gets pulled into the atmosphere—her inhibitions fall away, and her sensuality is on full display. Her moves are even more provocative than in the Spring Dance where she was somewhat inhibited by the large town gathering. Now she is dancing for Ramey, his family, and for herself. Some of the female cousins are surprised and the younger ones stare with open mouths and wide smiles. There is no doubt—she is *Dancing Girl*. Her detractors whisper how scandalous it is.

A few weeks after the dance, Ramey again brings up his plans for travel and she reluctantly resigns herself to the separation but tries to drive a firm bargain.

"On one condition, Ramey. As soon as you return, we will get married."

"Agreed," he says so quickly she is a little suspicious.

"I am going away just this one time and it will be short."

"Short? One month is not short."

Whenever Ramey speaks about this faraway kingdom with palaces and temples, there is a gleam in his eyes, as if he is in love with the idea, even though he does not know what these words mean. Zara is beginning to be afraid this faraway place may become a rival for his love.

She does not want to lose Ramey. She has heard other stories about the kingdom—of wars and cruelty and inequality—from people who do not think highly of the place. She is told that after Ramey's trip west, there will be no need to keep the super gems a secret. At least that would be one less family secret for her to hide. Ramey is trying to make Zara visualize things even he himself has never seen. She realizes he is not going to rest until he travels there, visits the empire, and satisfies himself about the truth. She finally agrees for him to take the trip west.

CHAPTER 3

Lightning Strikes Twice

Six months have passed since the beginning of Ramey and Zara's romance. Summer is over and the mild cool breezes from the northern plateaus are beginning to replace the hot dusty winds from the eastern desert. Soon it will be cool enough for early evening gatherings and the season for weddings and parties will begin.

Zara is well liked by Ramey's family and now eager to set a wedding date and go through the ceremony. Ramey understands her urgency. Ever since her exquisite performance at the Spring Dance when she became known as *Dancing Girl*, her family has received several enquiries about her availability for marriage. Ramey's family learns of these proposals through the town's gossip network.

Ramey's female cousins constantly needle him. Two of them take a seat near him in the courtyard and take out their colorful balls of yarn and begin knitting.

"I heard Zara turned down a proposal from a young man from a weaver family," one of them says, making sure Ramey is within hearing range.

Her companion is making wads of white cotton to start spinning more yarn. "Yes, yes. I also heard that. Zara is going to regret it. He is so handsome. I wish he would send a proposal for me."

"Her fame won't last forever. By the next Spring Festival there will be a new dancing girl and everyone will forget about this year's *Dancing Girl*."

"I wonder who she is waiting for, wasting her youth like this."

Ramey is incensed. "Don't you girls have anything better to do than to gossip all day?"

They giggle and run away, jangling their ankle bracelets.

"Why can't we set a date now?" Zara asks Ramey one day.

He struggles to explain the reason but tries anyway. "As I told you, Uncle and I are going west to sell the gold-streaked lapis necklaces."

"Why don't we get married and then you can go."

"It is a long trip. I don't want you to be alone."

"Well then, why don't you go and get it over with." She is right. If his trip stands in the way of their nuptials, then he should make the trip so they can get on with their life together.

He tries to explain. "Uncle has not been feeling well. As soon as he improves a little, he and I will leave."

Zara had not been aware of this new condition. The uncle coughs sometimes, but all old people have some coughing maladies, so she does not think much of it. Whenever she brings up Ramey's journey and his uncle's health, she is told Uncle is now taking a new decoction and is improving. Until they get married, she has to keep making excuses to her family every time a proposal comes in and fend off advances from young men in town.

And then a strange and very unpleasant incident takes place. Ramey is in the marketplace at a food stall, enjoying a snack of freshly fried fritters, dipping them alternately in a fragrant mint and a tart tamarind sauce, when he sees Zara's father, Dogar, coming out of a shop after conducting some business. He does not notice Ramey. Not wanting to be rude by ignoring him, Ramey puts the snack down, stands up and addresses him.

"Greetings sir. How are you?"

Dogar, completely wrapped up in his thoughts, takes a few moments to recognize Ramey. He speaks very curtly, bordering on a rebuke.

"How I am? Why do you ask? Do you think I am not well?"

Dogar

Ramey is taken aback. "No, no. I want to know how you are."

"Why in the world do you think you will be able to take care of my daughter? She is so immature and spoiled."

Ramey stutters, "Sir, I will try my . . ."

"Try? That is all? Well young man, that is not good enough. I don't think this is going to work out. You are not capable of taking care of her. Do you know how much effort and expense it takes to support her? Obviously, you don't."

Ramey makes another attempt at a polite answer, "Sir, we will do our best and . . ."

"That is all I keep hearing from you. Nothing very convincing."

Ramey's mind is in a swirl while Dogar carries on berating him, but Ramey cannot hear anything, let alone understand what has brought all this on. He has always been respectful to this man and has tried his best to behave honorably towards their family. Pride and anger swell up in him, but the thought of Zara suppresses anything unpleasant.

Dogar becomes angrier, belittling him by bringing up irrelevant incidents and calls him worthless. Ramey looks at him in surprise and bafflement. Dogar goes on to bring up imaginary faults in Zara. In his hurt and pain, Ramey cannot listen to him any longer. As soon as Dogar stops talking, Ramey leaves.

He is confused about the incident and has such difficulty processing it that he does not tell Zara about the conversation. He continues seeing her, but outside her father's presence. Even then, every time he sees her, her father's abusive words echo in his head and affect his countenance and the warmth of his words. Zara senses a cooling off from him, but she believes he is busy, and preoccupied with his work and the upcoming trip.

Ramey has been invited to a feast at Zara's house for which he cannot wait. He wants to see what if anything Dogar might say to him—if not an apology for his harsh abuse, at least some kind words. The evening commences. A sumptuous meal is served, and guests are enjoying the gathering. Dogar meets Ramey with a formal politeness but never displays any affection or even kindness, nor does he express any regret or apology. Ramey is so disgusted and disappointed he cannot taste the food, loses his appetite, and stops eating. He believes Dogar's feelings towards him have not changed and it would now be fruitless to pursue the relationship with Zara.

"Your father does not like me. He will not approve of our union."

Zara cannot understand why Ramey thinks her father does not like him.

"You don't really believe it. He has always been so kind to you. Don't you remember those long discussions you two had comparing the selling of jewelry and cloth?"

"I remember those very well and that is why I don't understand the change in him." Ramey looks puzzled and deeply worried.

Unable to convince him, Zara keeps trying but he continues to resist. Their conversations used to be about their lives together, their future plans, and their love for each other. Now whenever they are together, they spend most of the time arguing about her father. Ramey still has strong romantic feelings towards her, but it is now a sad love—as if he is about to leave her and is saying his goodbyes.

She sets out to uncover her father's attitude towards Ramey. Over time Ramey has become so well accepted and completely trusted by her family, there are no restrictions on her meetings with him. She is allowed to spend as much time as she wants. Now she wants to test her father to see if he approves of this arrangement. When she finishes her chores, she makes sure her father is nearby and says to no one in particular, "I am going to go see Ramey." She steals a glance at her father to see if he notices what she is saying. He looks up from the swatches of cloth he is examining, with an alarmed expression. Rather than immediately walking out, she lingers to see his reaction. His attention is still on her as she is about to step out of the house.

"Do you have to go?" he says.

She pauses, turns around and faces him, "Yes, Baba, did you want me to do something?"

He looks conflicted, "I mean do you have to go right now?"

"I can wait. When else did you want me to go see Ramey?"

He eventually relents, but she is aware of a shift in his attitude. In the past there would have been no reaction from him, if he even paid attention to what she was saying.

Zara repeats this test every day for the next week and notices a gradual but definite hardening of her father's attitude. On the fifth day, he tells her not to see Ramey and wait until the next day. When she tries to probe further, he shuts down. Puzzled, she senses not so much a definite reason for his change in attitude, but rather a closing up, as if he is afraid to discuss his feelings. She can see he has no hostility towards Ramey, but rather a fear of the unknown. Rather than bringing it out in the open and discussing it, he prefers to let their relationship lapse like a plant that dries up when not watered.

Zara is thrown into a state of confusion. She cannot understand what has happened to turn her dream of a lifelong romantic future with Ramey into a nightmare. Now, she dreads each morning for what new disappointments it might bring. One night she dreams she is drowning in the river. The water reaches high monsoon level—the rushing river turns into a succession of swirling whirlpools, rushing eddies and cresting waves. Zara has been afraid of water since she was a child and her calves had cramped up while swimming with other children. She felt like the current was pulling her under—and then the real horror began. In the dream, she sees her father standing on the bank looking across the river to the other bank. She calls out to him for help, and he momentarily looks in her direction. But there is no recognition in his face. Either he does not see her, or does not recognize her, or does not realize what is happening to her. He continues to stare across the river toward the other bank.

The nightmare deepens as Zara glances at the other bank to see what her father is looking at and realizes it is Ramey. She calls out to him, but he also ignores her and keeps staring back at her father. She feels like she is about to go under for the last time when she wakes up in a cold sweat, tears flowing down her face. It is almost daybreak. She gets up from bed shaking. Afraid and weak, she has a fever into the night. She slowly recovers and in a few days feels better. Then her nightmare repeats. This time there is a log floating by, and she manages to grab it and begins to come up. She gets a clearer look at both her father and Ramey glaring at each other, oblivious to her distress. The nightmares keep recurring with new horrors each time. One time a fierce animal, a cross between a wolf and a bear, floats by and she tries to grab its tail to stay afloat. The animal snarls and swipes at her with a claw causing a painful wound and waking her up.

Her family knows she is having bad dreams as she wakes up sobbing, screaming or crying. At the same time, Dogar has been traveling to Mohenjo-Daro and beyond for his trading trips selling the colorful high-end cloth. Dogar decides they will leave Harappa and move to Mohenjo-Daro, apparently for business reasons, but also thinking Zara might improve with distance from Ramey and the places she associates with romance and love. Zara urges Ramey for the last time to approach her father and ask for her hand. Ramey tells her he is convinced her father will not accept his suit. She is heartbroken and descends into a bout of depression, refusing to come out of their house. Soon after, when Dogar and his family leave town, Ramey and Zara lose all contact with each other.

The distraction caused by the move to another town works for Zara for a while. The preoccupation with a new location suppresses her nightmares. Dogar starts trading in metals and regularly travels to Mesopotamia. There he discovers temples, priests, and scholars trained in the arts of spiritual, mental and physical healing. He decides to take Zara with him to find a cure for her ailment, which is affecting her body, her mind, and her spirit. His amateur praying to the Goddess has not worked, but the higher arts of the priests of the temple at Ur might help her.

Ramey's world has been turned upside down. He has no interest in taking a trip to any kingdom and begins neglecting his usual jewelry making duties. His family is worried about the change in his condition. Uncle Banzil's cough persists. One day when he is feeling a little better, he calls Ramey to his bedside.

"Well Ramey, we need to sell our super bead jewelry."

"Uncle, who would buy those? No one in Indus can afford them."

"Do you still remember what I had told you about the river valley out west?"

"The rich valley? Where people will pay a lot for our super gems?"

"The same, with kings and palaces and temples."

"When you feel a little better, we will go there together."

"Not likely," his uncle says and shakes his head.

Ramey can see the despair in his eyes. Is uncle giving up on life? He is in a pensive mood.

"Have you ever been to the eastern desert, Ramey?"

"Yes uncle. I have gone past the Ghaggar-Hakra River, but not very far."

"Did you ever see a mirage?"

"No, but I've heard about them and was warned to not try and reach one."

With a deep sigh, Uncle says, "I feel I have been chasing mirages all my life. But this time I have a good feeling about the trip to the kingdom of two rivers. It won't be another mirage."

"As I said Uncle, when you feel better, we will both go there."

Banzil looks somber. "Start getting ready but keep the destination to yourself. And remember to guard the secret of how a drill made from soft bronze can drill through a hard gemstone like lapis. This should remain our family's secret. It is our pathway to greater wealth and distinction in the community."

Uncle Banzil's cough keeps getting worse, but no one thinks it is life threatening. He is being treated using decoctions made with village-grown herbs, but there is no improvement. People suggest other remedies—for his lungs, his heart, or his liver. One man who collects herbs in the forest says it is his stomach. His treatment seems to improve Uncle's condition a little, but he never completely gets well, and the cough continues. In his frustration Uncle Banzil turns to someone who claims to summon the spirits who can cure him, but nothing makes the cough go away. He finally turns to magic and to a woman who claims to heal by having a strong faith but nobody knows in what.

On a warm day in August, and even though he feels tired, Uncle leaves his bed and works all day, teaching Ramey how to grade gems. His vigor and enthusiasm have returned, and his face has a glow not seen in some time. Ramey leaves for an errand and upon his return finds his uncle back in the store room fussing over some gems, looking for the gold-streaked lapis.

"We are not done with work, Ramey," he says.

Ramey has had enough of a lesson for one day. "We can finish this tomorrow, Uncle."

Uncle is holding some gems in his hand with a bright look on his face. "Here is the gold-streaked lapis. See, see?"

"I have seen these." Ramey says. "Let's eat first, Uncle." What is the big hurry after all.

When they sit down to dinner, Uncle nibbles at the food, says it is tasteless, and gets up. While

Ramey is still eating his dinner, he hears a gurgling sound, thinking Uncle is doing his ablutions for the evening *puja*.

Suddenly, Uncle screams, "Ramey, I can't breathe."

Ramey jumps up, runs to him and sees him vomiting dark red blood. Ramey realizes blood of this color must be from an internal organ, not a shallow wound or cut. He grabs Uncle around his waist to help him spit it out. Uncle vomits some more blood and goes limp in his arms. Ramey shouts for help and two of the cousins come running. One rubs Uncle's arms, the other massages his chest. One of Uncle's daughters appears and starts praying and uttering incantations. Another daughter cries while Auntie wails loudly. The family tries their best, but to no avail. Uncle is dead. Soon his body begins to get cold.

It takes several days for the family to complete the funeral and mourning period but even longer to comprehend the loss. The family is in shock and saddened. Ramey's moroseness deepens.

The matter of selling the gold-streaked lapis lazuli super beads or a trip to the kingdom of two rivers is no longer discussed. Family members begin adjusting to life without Uncle, but Ramey is unable to tend to his daily duties. A year passes before he finally begins participating in the jewelry business, though very listlessly. Another year goes by when finally they are able to convince Ramey to go to sell the super beads. Ramey shows some enthusiasm. The family encourages him partly for business reasons, but also hoping the trip will rejuvenate him.

Almost three years since his separation from Zara and Uncle Banzil's death, Ramey prepares to travel.

River Boats on the Dock

CHAPTER 4

Downriver Journey

On this chilly morning, the passengers huddle near the riverbank waiting for the boat to pull up to the dock. The dock is a brick structure dug into the shallow riverbed along the bank. A brick wall juts into the river, creating a smooth backwater for loading and unloading. The passengers express concern over the delay.

One of the cousins has come to see Ramey off. Ramey notices a young man glancing repeatedly in their direction.

"Who is that?" he asks his cousin.

"Who? Where?"

"The young man over there in the red cap."

It takes his cousin a few moments to spot the red cap in a cluster of five men. A young man about 16 years old with a medium build holds his *khes* wrap awkwardly, shifting it from one shoulder to the other. His upper torso is disproportionality long, which gives him the stature of a tall person, but with his short legs he is barely average height. His baby face resembles an oddly made doll or puppet. The cousin searches his memory for an image to match the young man's appearance. Finally, recognition shows in his eyes.

"He is the son of a farmer I know, but he's grown so much. Let me ask him."

Before Ramey can stop him, he motions the young man to come over. Hesitant at first, his cousin waves to him again and the boy walks over.

"You are Karing's son, aren't you?" The boy has a guilty expression, as if he's been caught doing something wrong. "What are you doing so far from home?" The cousin speaks sternly as if questioning a younger brother. The young man looks perplexed. "Are you lost?"

The boy looks embarrassed and clearly offended. He gathers his courage and clears his throat. "I am not lost."

The cousin keeps looking at him, waiting for an answer to his first question.

The young man points to an older man standing with three other men, who is now staring in his direction. "I am helping the cloth merchant."

At first glance, a jolt goes through Ramey's body—it is Zara's father. Soon after Dogar insulted him and discouraged him from even proposing to his love, the girl and her family left town. Ramey has not heard anything further about them in the last three years. The cousin is busy talking to the young man, so he does not notice the tension building in Ramey's face.

"The cloth merchant has a heavy bundle of clothing," says the boy. "Our harvest is done, so my father arranged this for me."

"You know my cousin Ramey. He will be traveling on the same boat."

The boy looks at Ramey as if to memorize his face.

"What is your name?" Ramey asks.

"Karoi."

"Karoi, your friends are beginning to wonder." Ramey waves him back to his party

The young man goes back and answers questions from the others who keep sneaking a look at Ramey and his cousin. Ramey understands that an older cloth trader would require help from younger shoulders to carry his merchandise.

When the boat is ready to depart, the cousin notices the expression on Ramey's face. "Are you feeling all right?"

Ramey tries to cover up. "Yes, yes, I am fine—just thinking about the boat travel."

The cousin is not convinced but it is almost time for the boat to leave the dock and for him to go home. Ramey is not pleased at the prospect of sharing the boat ride with cruel Dogar, the cloth trader.

Earlier, the waiting passengers stood near a copse of trees shielded from the cold morning chill. Each passenger has a bundle he will place under the bench seat. Some carry a thick cotton *khes* (a blanket-sized shawl), which serves as their protection against weather, as an outer garment for display, a seat cover for comfort and a light blanket during sleep. As the boat pulls away, a couple of passengers stand up and wrap the cotton *khes* around their shoulders to stay warm against the morning fog hanging over the water. The colorful border of each cotton blanket is distinct, and the colors give a hint of the social status, community group, and perhaps even the profession of each traveler. Most of the blanket borders are in earth tones of various shades and darkness, with a couple in blue or green hues. Ramey's *khes* with a finely tinted dark tan border and matching tassels, along with his shiny brown leather *khussa* shoes, stand out amongst the travelers.

Once out on the open water, it is colder and the fog denser. The woodsy fragrance of leafy

Downriver Journey

trees from the riverbank is replaced with the rush of subtle aromas the river is dragging along in its current from upriver—the scent of damp earth from a marshy bank, a decaying stench of algae from a backwater channel, and the resinous whiff of pines from the distant plateau.

During downriver trips, the crew must be alert and focused, but it does not take much strenuous effort. If they manage to keep the boat away from any snags such as logs stuck in the mud and sand shoals, the trip is considered successful. One of the crewmembers watches out for obstructions and keeps warning the active rower in a subdued monotone to steer one way or the other to avoid danger. Soon the passengers are lulled by the gentle murmur of eddies and currents and settle down in comfortable postures.

After two hours on the river and the sun's arrival, the fog lifts and passengers begin to stir. Ramey is sitting across from Dogar and Karoi. Dogar tries a couple of times to make eye contact with Ramey, but Ramey avoids him. With this seating arrange-ment it is impossible to avoid him for very long, so when Dogar smiles at him, Ramey gives a terse shake of his head in acknowledgement. Karoi does not know anyone other than Ramey, so he scoots over closer to him.

"Is this your first time in a boat?" Ramey asks.

There is uncertainty in the boy's face, "No, no. Not the first."

"Have you been far?"

"Well," Karoi says, "not far."

"They are quite safe. I have been on boats many times."

Just then, the boat crosses a small, fast whirlpool with a sharp jolt, nearly going into a spin. Karoi's hands grip the gunwale tightly. Ramey suppresses a grin and resumes his words of encouragement. He points to a large clay water pot, a *ghara*, under the rower's bench.

These large clay pots are used to carry and store water. They keep the water cool during the summer months with steady evaporation through their porous sides.

"Do you know what that is?" Ramey asks.

Karoi's face shows slight scorn at the condescending question.

"Yes, everyone knows."

Ramey realizes the boy is beginning to resent their encounter and decides to switch to a gentler approach. He points to a couple of clay water pots stored under other bench seats.

"There are a few of these—"

Karoi sees an opening and looks around triumphantly at the flowing river. "If we ever get thirsty."

"Yes, these also help us swim across water."

Karoi has a blank look, so Ramey grabs one *ghara* pot, puts his right arm around its neck, and swings his left arm back and forth, as if paddling in water. Karoi looks appreciative and Ramey feels he has relieved the young man's anxiety somewhat.

Dogar has been listening to them with a bemused expression and tries to initiate a conversation

"How have you been, Ramey?"

"I have been fine," Ramey says, and looks away. He cannot forget how this man so vehemently opposed his suit to Zara and wants to say something harsh but controls himself.

What does he want, Ramey wonders. Why is he trying to engage in a conversation with me? Their last encounter three years back had been so bitter that Ramey can still feel the gall in his throat. A vague image of Zara floats across his mind. He wonders what has happened to her—but keeps it to himself.

The mid-day sun is now overhead as their journey continues. The boat has been underway for about six hours. The currents are fast in this stretch of the river and there are many bends and turns.

By this time, the passengers have experienced several whirlpools, eddies, near misses with logs, and other snags. The two rowers manning the boat have expertly dealt with every circumstance and the passengers have come to depend on the two as skillful and competent. As they traverse a bend in the river, the boat goes through a swirling whirlpool. It takes a sharp turn into an abandoned old channel, runs straight into a sand shoal, and promptly gets stuck with a loud thud along its bottom. The strong jolt wakes up the passengers who have dozed off under their *khes* blankets. Ramey, with his trader's eye for reading people's faces and expressions, looks at the two-man crew and senses concern in their faces. Either this is a situation neither of the rowers has ever dealt with or what has happened is serious.

He leaves the young man and the cloth trader, gets up and walks over to one of the rowers with a quizzical look. The worried expression on the face of the rower does not change. Ramey notices the other rower who has been in support mode for the last couple of hours has taken his shoes off and is busy hiking up his *lungi* sarong wrap above his knees. Apparently, he intends to step out of the boat onto the sandbank and try and push the boat back into the main channel. Ramey sees an expression on the face of the other rower indicating he is not sure this approach will work.

Surely, Ramey thinks, this can't be the first time they have faced this kind of predicament. To his surprise, upon checking, neither of the two has been in a situation where the boat had gotten stuck in a dead-end channel. This is not a one-man job, Ramey thinks, and one of the rowers must remain in the boat. He looks at his new *khussa* shoes and his freshly washed *lungi*, takes a deep breath and slips off his shoes. As he stands up and begins hiking up his *lungi*, he looks at Karoi.

"Well friend, you are going to have your first lesson in river travel."

"What?" Karoi does not grasp his meaning.

"We have to help get the boat out."

"Oh," he says as he also removes his shoes and hikes up his *lungi*. The first rower is already outside the boat standing in knee-deep water on the marshy mud shoal. Ramey steps out, followed by Karoi. The rower has grabbed the bow of the boat. He jerks it side to side to try to figure out at what point on the bottom it is hung up. The limited to and fro movement is not enough to discern the boat's contact point, so Ramey helps the rower gradually enlarge the range of motion. With each push their feet sink deeper into the clay layer over the sand bar. It takes a greater effort to ignore the sticky feeling around their feet, then ankles and now calves. They churn up the wet earth until the water around them looks murky. Ramey cannot see the river bottom even though the water is only up to his thighs. The smell of wet mud rises becoming stronger with each movement of their feet. Ramey has seen potters and brick makers knead wet clay with their feet and often wondered what it feels like. Now he knows.

After moving the boat through half a dozen cycles, it is clear the fulcrum is dead center—the hardest part to free.

"What shall we do?" Karoi asks.

"It is the middle," Ramey says.

"Is that good?"

"No, it is bad. We both have to push."

Karoi tries pushing the boat in vain. Ramey also joins in following commands from the rower.

"Ready, ready, heave," and after a pause, "Ready, ready, push."

The alternate pushing and heaving by the three men finally breaks it free from the sticky river bottom. After about ten coordinated pushes, the boat is afloat again.

"Get in, get in!" the rower shouts with urgency. The water is getting deeper at a rapid rate and soon will be too deep to walk. Both Karoi and Ramey make it into the boat just in time, but the rower has to swim a few strokes while hanging onto the boat to push it into the main channel. He times his climb over the gunwale perfectly. One leg is still in the air when the boat takes off at a rapid speed.

Some of the passengers thank them while they are still coming over the gunwale, while others wait until they make eye contact to thank them. It takes Ramey and Karoi a few minutes to arrange their clothes, wipe their feet and gather themselves. Ramey clearly had the lead role in freeing the boat, but Karoi supplied plenty of muscle. Dogar addresses Ramey, but Ramey pretends not to notice him and keeps talking to a passenger on the other side.

Their journey continues into the late afternoon, and just before sunset, they stop for the night and unload their possessions. A short walk away is an adobe building with an enclosed courtyard. A family who runs the place greets them and the wife begins preparing a meal. The food is served, and mats provided for the night.

As the sun goes down, darkness emanates from the thick jungle. The passengers prepare to settle down for the night in a space created by clearing a small portion of the adjacent forest. Ramey senses the nocturnal creatures preparing for their nightly excursions. The odors coming from the forest are not simply those of vegetation, but a medley of animal smells mixed with trees and shrubs.

Ramey initially sees the innkeeper has assigned Dogar a mat a couple of spaces away, but the travelers in the middle want to sleep inside, so the cloth trader ends up right next to him. Ramey tries to control his bitterness as he thinks of the past. He is tempted to inquire about Zara, but his disdain for this man is too much. Soon the exhaustion from the boat rescue overtakes him and he drifts off to sleep.

CHAPTER 5

An Old Memory

The innkeeper is testy. "You should have told me before you started eating. You already ate, now you tell me you cannot pay," he says to a farmer and his wife. They came from the boat yesterday, ate dinner last night, spent the night at his lodging, and had breakfast this morning. The farmer looks around awkwardly as the innkeeper raises his voice so everyone in the courtyard can hear him.

The farmer decides to be firm. "If the boat had not gotten stuck, we could have been on our way last night—not in this hovel."

"Hovel? This is a hovel to you? What palace have you been living in?"

Confused, the farmer looks around to see if others understand the innkeeper's meaning. "What are you talking about? A palace?"

There are a few snickers around the courtyard. Evidently the farmer has not traveled far.

"A palace is where the king lives." The innkeeper tries to keep a straight face, but a smile escapes his lips. The farmer now knows the innkeeper is baiting him and his temper rises.

"Who are you calling a king? You yourself are probably a king?"

The innkeeper laughs as do some of the others. Ramey is reclining on a mat on his *khes* blanket. Noticing the farmer's predicament, he decides it is enough. He tells the innkeeper to add the farm couple's meal and night's stay to his account. And the argument ends.

The farmer and his wife nod appreciatively at Ramey. It is true the couple had no intention of staying overnight at the inn. Had the boat made it to this stop earlier in the day, they would have walked for a couple of hours to the home of the wife's parents. Ramey thinks he has seen the farmer around Harappa, but the wife is clearly from one of the smaller settlements nearby. He sympathizes with them.

"I never wanted to come on the boat," the farmer says, speaking to no one, but within Ramey's hearing, as if to explain their situation. "I could have walked this far and more easily." And that is true, most of the travel in the Indus Valley is on foot trails along the riverbanks.

"It is not easy for me," the wife speaks up, "it would take us three days. My mother is sick, so we are in a hurry." They feel they have laid it all out for their benefactor, pick up their belongings and slip away.

Coming from a town surrounded by farmland, Ramey rarely spends a night this close to a forest and is overwhelmed with the scents and sounds all around. When everything from birds to small animals and tree leaves finally announce the morning, he packs up his things, clears his account, and heads out to the boat.

All those who are traveling further downriver board with him. As they get underway, the nature of vegetation, along with the colors and scents of their surroundings, begins to change from leafy, green deciduous trees with a woodsy smell, to arid-zone succulent flora with needle-shaped leaves and a muted aroma.

Ramey notices that Dogar again tries to make eye contact, so he offers a lukewarm acknowledgment, and then looks off in the direction they are heading. Some of his bitterness has begun to melt away.

"I heard about your Uncle Banzil's death," the cloth trader says.

Ramey hesitates before responding. He maintains a stern expression even though any mention of his deceased uncle touches him deeply.

"Yes, Uncle Banzil died three years ago," Ramey says in a direct manner.

Dogar scoots over closer to Ramey.

"Very sad, very sad."

"Well, it was very sudden."

"Sad, very sad," Dogar says, "I have been living in Mohenjo-Daro."

Ramey wants to ask about Zara, but does not know how to bring it up, so simply makes small talk.

"How difficult are the summers there?"

"About the same as in Harappa—only longer. And there is no relief with the monsoon rains. But I have been spending a lot of time in the mountains, opening new mines in search of ores."

"How difficult are summers in the mountains?"

"Difficulty is in winter. It is very cold and dry. The dryness hurts the skin and the cold hurts the bones, even though there is not much snow".

"Snow?" Ramey has seen water drops that freeze and fall as hail, but never snow. He thinks it best to keep the conversation on an easy topic like weather.

"Ah, yes, snow," Dogar turns wistful. "It is beautiful, like a soft white blanket. It covers trees, rocks, ground, houses—everything."

"And the hill people? Do they also get covered?"

Dogar smiles, "If they keep standing outside."

Ramey is not sure what that means, but it is not important. He is not planning to travel to the western mountains.

"How are the mountain people? They must be different?"

Dogar seems to be focusing somewhere far away. When he speaks, he sounds distant.

"Hardy, tough, unforgiving, but very loyal. Willing to die for a friend."

Ramey is trying to digest this new array of personal qualities.

"They are always ready to fight—and to kill, if necessary," Dogar says as if warning him.

Ramey makes a mental note to avoid a quarrel with anyone from the mountains. He has avoided any mention of the events of nearly three years ago, but that does not stop Dogar.

"It has been a big regret of my life how I rebuffed your advances towards my daughter."

Ramey does not care about Dogar's regrets or his feelings. He has enough of his own painful memories, but Dogar is intent on talking. Ramey remains quiet, as Dogar goes on.

"Perhaps it was my false pride, my ignorance, or my ill luck. I do not know what to call it. You were a very eligible and presentable young man, and I belittled you. I cannot explain why I did that. Perhaps, as they say, when the Goddess wants to destroy someone, she takes away his senses. I did not need her help, or curse, I did it all myself. You tolerated and withstood my stupid comments and still maintained relationships with us—you even gave me a second chance," Dogar's voice trembles.

Ramey looks away. He does not know whether to pity him or hate him. After a few moments Dogar resumes his confession.

"In some ways, you are like me—unassuming, not boastful—waiting to be recognized and valued on your own merits, not because you claim to be great. I treated you poorly and ignored you. To this day, I remember the moment when you and I were sitting face to face during the feast at our house. I remember the look in your eyes waiting to be acknowledged. I hesitated in case others might hear my apologies. And just like that, the moment was gone. I missed the last chance to make up with you and redeem myself."

Dogar chokes up. Ramey feels awkward and looks down the river, "I think we are getting close to our destination."

Dogar does not hear him and continues in his trance-like recollection, "At the moment when I admired you greatly, I hesitated. I was waiting for you to ask for my blessing. But in light of my past comments, you justifiably waited for me to initiate the conversation, to reassure you that you would not be dismissed again. Neither of us said anything, and the occasion was lost due to my hesitation."

Dogar's eyes are moist—he is overcome with emotion. Ramey stays quiet and Dogar does not even notice him anymore. Dogar turns inward, living in a hell of his own making, which he keeps stoked so his punishment is meted out at the most intense level of suffering. Perhaps the Goddess will soothe his heart or maybe punish him further for causing pain to others. Ramey does not want to think about it.

There is no further conversation until the boat ride comes to an end. They get off at their destination. Spent and subdued, Dogar hurries away after a brief good-bye, followed by his young helper Karoi carrying the large bundle on his shoulders. Ramey stands on the dock thinking wistfully of Zara. But he does not allow himself the luxury of dreaming what might have been. He knows invariably that will lead to more pain. He was waiting for Dogar to mention her name, but he did not. She must have suffered as much as Ramey, if not more. He wonders how she bears it—if indeed she has.

Ramey looks around at the dock and turns his thoughts to his surroundings. He has now reached Mohenjo-Daro, the southern town in the Indus Valley. He stretches and takes a deep breath, absorbing the distinct scents of the town. Different earth materials, minerals and vegetation produce an aroma all their own. Windy, dry and dusty, the arid region vegetation looks stunted to Ramey who is used to the open fertile plains, rich with flora. This town is as hot as Harappa, but outside the monsoon zone, so it has a baked odor with deeper but subdued scents, as if the rocky earth and the desert vegetation must inwardly toughen themselves. Ramey picks up his bundle and heads out towards town.

CHAPTER 6

River Indus to the Sea

Walking to his friend Berum's house, Ramey reminds himself what he is about to see in this southern center of the Indus Valley. He comes from an egalitarian northern town where social distinctions are frowned upon. Here in Mohenjo-Daro everything from pottery to clothing, to one's house is an item of distinction. His friend Berum has tried to school him in recognizing and appreciating articles of social status, but much of the effort is lost on Ramey. One thing Ramey has learned is that the market for his gem necklaces and beads is much better in this status-conscious city than in his own hometown that frowns on such symbols. He also knows that what he is selling is meant for a richer place and is quite beyond the means of anyone even in this town.

He arrives at his friend's house in late afternoon. After their early evening meal, they sit down to chat and relax before turning in for the night. Ramey needs to sit upright for some time until the food has settled—the only way to prevent heartburn from the spicy food. He is always struck by the number of spices used in cooking in this southern part of Indus Valley. Perhaps because of the year-round warm weather, they need more seasoning to prevent their food from spoiling. The food is much tastier, but the flavor and aroma come at a cost—tongue-biting heat and stomach-churning aftereffects.

"What are the new gems this time?" Berum asks. "Two summers back you brought rainbow beads. They were very popular at our Spring Festival."

Ramey shakes his head, "Nothing. I am not selling anything in Mohenjo-Daro this time."

"So, are you going into the farm country? The farmers will not buy your fancy gems."

"I am not going to the farm country either."

"To the mountains then. I hear the tribes have been fighting again."

"Thanks for the warning. I have heard the same thing."

"Where to then?"

Ramey puts on a serious expression, so he is believed.

"Downriver."

Berum is quiet for a few moments, but the surprise shows on his face.

"There is nothing downriver except the delta marshes with some fishermen."

Ramey looks directly into his friend's eyes, "There is something. There is a port."

"A port? That is the sea. I have never heard of anyone from Harappa going out to sea."

"My Uncle Banzil had always wanted to, but he died before he could."

Berum looks contemplative, "How did he die?"

"Very suddenly. Some say it was poison. Others say it was a curse from the Goddess."

Berum ponders. "Your family knows where you are going?"

"My family knows, but people in Harappa think I am with you."

"What should I say if someone asks since you obviously won't be here."

"Tell them I am in the back country hunting wild boars. No, that sounds too dangerous. Quail. I'll be hunting quail."

"Quail? Will you bring any quail when you return?"

"No, I am not a good hunter. No quail."

Berum's thoughts are on the next day. "If you are going on a sea voyage, tomorrow we should go see a man who knows a lot about salt water."

"Salt water?"

"Yes, the sea is filled with it." Berum says, "You did not know?"

"I was hoping you knew someone like that in Mohenjo-Daro."

The next day Ramey and Berum go to the house of an experienced seafarer in the northern outskirts of Mohenjo-Daro, further away from the river. Ramey is not used to the uphill climb as his hometown is in a flat plain. But there is a reward at the end of the hilly trek—a panoramic view of the whole town. Ramey wonders what his hometown might look like if he could ever fly up this high, but he dismisses the idea as an idle thought.

Archeological Site, Indus Valley Town

They are shown into a sitting room and told to wait. Ramey notices an unusual item on a wall—a parchment map. He stands up to examine it but cannot grasp its various geographic features. He assumes the blue must be water, but it is much wider than any river he has ever seen—even wider than the Indus. The sketches of hills with white peaks remind him that mountains have snow.

"This is the world you will be going into," the host says as he enters the room, "This is the kingdom of two rivers."

Ramey hears the voice and turns around to face Dogar, who has a confused expression as he recognizes Ramey. Berum did not tell him who he was bringing with him. Ramey wishes he had asked the name of this seafarer before coming. He has a flash of Zara and wonders if she is in this house.

Dogar attempts a smile. "Your friend has not told me anything about your destination."

"That is right," Berum says, "because I have not been told anything by my friend."

Dogar composes himself first, as if he sees a chance to atone for his past behavior. "I know," he says, "when a man from Harappa wants to know about salt water, he must have the kingdom of two rivers on his mind."

Dogar's high forehead and bright, intelligent eyes make people pay attention to what he is about to say. The way he carries himself exudes confidence. Trying to overcome the awkwardness of the meeting, Ramey sits down wondering if Zara is going to come in. As time goes by and there is no sign of her, his thoughts turn to his upcoming journey.

"Ramey is a good friend of mine," Berum says, "and he wants to see the Outworld beyond the Indus Valley."

Dogar looks at Ramey with the hint of a smile, "Have you ever traveled downriver of Mohenjo-Daro?"

Ramey shakes his head.

"How about beyond the mountains out west?"

Ramey shakes his head again. Although he has taken over the trader duties from his uncle, he has only travelled to locations within the Indus Valley, except occasional trips to meet couriers bringing minerals from the eastern desert or gems from the northern mountains. He wants to talk about all the places his uncle traveled to but thinks it would sound like an idle boast.

"I have been bringing ore from the western mountains and selling it in the valley of the two rivers," Dogar says, explaining his knowledge of sea travel. He shifts his gaze out the window over the town spread out below the bluff. He can see well beyond as he retraces his travel routes in his mind, "The sea is big. Very big."

"And salty," Ramey says, displaying his newly acquired knowledge.

Dogar laughs, "Yes, very salty, so don't drink from it."

"I have tasted water from brackish wells before." Ramey wants Dogar to know he is not totally ignorant. He may not have ever gone south of Mohenjo-Daro, but he knows of the world.

Dogar shakes his head, "You have never tasted anything like the seawater." He settles back in his seat willing to spend some time tutoring Ramey. As he is one of the few people in the Indus Valley who has made several trips to the sea, Dogar enjoys recounting his experiences.

"I know you travel up and down the rivers often," Dogar continues.

"Yes, like Ravi, like the Indus," Ramey says.

Berum gives him a side glance, briefly holding up his index finger to his lips. He does not want his friend to interrupt the flow of Dogar's narrative. There will be time for questions and elaborations later.

"The sea is very different. I have been there eight to ten times. Each trip took one, sometimes two months. The uncertainty and hardship in each sea voyage equals ten river journeys."

"Do you know what a *dhow* is?" Dogar asks.

Ramey now knows not to speak and simply shakes his head.

"A *dhow* is a large boat. Four, maybe five river boats equal one *dhow*—and with sails. Do you know what sails are?"

"I have heard of sails," Ramey keeps it short.

"One other thing—soldiers and weapons—two things I had never seen before." Dogar realizes both the young men are puzzled. "Weapon, like a sword. A big knife to kill people—not animals. Soldiers are men who train and get paid for using a sword to kill people. It took me a few trips to understand this culture of kings, empires, soldiers and weapons. It is not as important to know these for trading but as a caution for your safety." Dogar goes on, "But we are honest traders, so soldiers and weapons and killings do not concern us. We speak the truth. We do not cheat, so we do not fear anyone." He thinks for a moment, "Except, except, those people who try to cheat simple traders like us."

"Cheat, how?'

"Many ways to cheat honest simple traders. 'I pay you tomorrow,' one will say. You go look for him tomorrow and he is gone. Left town. Or went into hiding and you cannot find him."

"Somebody would do that? But that is not right."

"In the kingdom it is done. If you trade, ask to see payment before you give them your wares. Otherwise, you will never see the payment. You will go home with empty hands."

Ramey shakes his head in disbelief. "In Harappa, one person did that five years ago. He was shamed by the whole community. He is no longer a trader."

Dogar sees Ramey's expression, the angle of his neck, and the brightness of his eyes that reflects the small-town Harappa pride.

"Makes no difference what kind of place you come from or how proud you are. You cannot eat pride. No matter how honest you are, you still need food and clothes, and a place to sleep. And remember the empire is powerful because they collect wealth and knowledge from people. If they see any unusual capability in their neighboring communities, they want to acquire it."

"And do they teach the neighboring communities also?"

"No, they protect their knowledge unless there is a cooperative exchange of it."

"Like trading."

"Exactly like trading. I will only let you take something of mine if you give me what I want from you." Dogar thinks he needs to give him something he can use. "I suggest two things. First thing, ask to see payment before you settle on the trade. Second, trade and payment should be at the same time. Ask for payment immediately—not in one hour, not in one day, not in one week—but at the same time."

"Sounds rude."

"Very rude, but this is the way the kingdom people are. Especially when dealing with out-of-town simple traders like us."

It is getting late, and their travel fatigue is catching up with them. Dogar needs to get back to his daily routine. Berum thanks Dogar for his hospitality and generosity in sharing information.

"One last thing," Dogar says to Ramey.

"Watch for informers and minders."

"Are they also dishonest traders?" Ramey thinks he has already received enough warning.

"They are not traders," says Dogar, "they are more dangerous."

Ramey tries to focus through his fatigue. "Who are these informers and minders?"

"They are spies. People in the village who listen to your private talk, then go and tell other people."

"I don't know anybody in the kingdom. So, who cares?"

"You must care—be careful. These spies will go tell the king."

"What does he care about a poor trader from the Indus?"

"If they think you are trying to harm the king."

"How can I harm the king?"

"That is exactly the kind of question that will get you into trouble. Don't say anything bad about the king, the empire or the temple. Don't ask questions about things that are not your business." Dogar wraps up their conversation. "Ramey. If there is something you want to know, only ask respectful questions. Think of the king as the head of a town council, with a big stick in his hand."

Ramey and his friend Berum thank Dogar and leave. Zara's name never comes up, nor does he see her or hear her voice. Perhaps she is happily married and living in her own house. Ramey pines for her in his memory.

As they walk back, Ramey ponders his upcoming journey to the kingdom of the two rivers. Vigilance, now his new watchword. Berum walks alongside.

"I met someone who came from Ur, the holy city in the kingdom of two rivers," Berum says with a smile. "He was boasting about the two wonders of the world they have. First—their temple where every prayer is granted. And second—their famous *Dancing Girl*, who also grants wishes."

Ramey's focuses his mind on his travels and the value of his gems. People value them as a means of saving, storing, and hiding wealth that can be easily and safely transported, and when needed, displayed as a show of status and vanity. After a few days' rest, he boards a boat heading downriver to the edge of the ocean. There he finds out a *dhow* will be leaving for Sumer in three days, so he decides to stay in an inn near the seaport.

CHAPTER 7

Voyage to the Empire

On the morning of departure, Ramey awakens early. The high humidity and the salty vapors from the ocean make his clothes sticky and his senses dull. After a tasteless meal of cereals made from unfamiliar grains and a bowl of warm greenish liquid, he is ready to go. The greenish liquid intrigues him—it suddenly wakes him up.

As he leaves the breakfast area, he asks the kitchen worker pouring the drink, "What is this?"

"What is this? It is a drink."

Ramey realizes he has not phrased the question accurately in the coastal dialect.

"How do you make it?"

"Ahh, that is what you mean. We boil it."

"Boil what?"

"This." The worker shows him a handful of small green beans. Ramey picks one up and smells it. There is no fragrance. He bites it but quickly spits it out.

"It is bitter," Ramey says with a contorted face.

The worker laughs. "Of course. What do you expect?"

"But my drink is sweet."

The worker swells with the pride of his creativity. "I made it sweet. I added licorice root for boiling."

Ramey has tasted licorice root before but does not recall any sensation of alertness. The worker sees his confusion.

"You feel awake? Yes? It is the green bean."

"Where do you get it?"

"Ahh. You want for yourself. Go to the other side of the gulf—in the hills of Yemen. A man from there brings it for us. He says it grows on the hills in his village. He always says he cannot wake up in this hot, humid place by the ocean. 'It makes me lazy. I need my green beans to wake me up.' But you cannot take it with you—four days it rots."

Whatever this stimulant is, it is not suitable for carrying with him. Ramey is thinking it might give him some advantage in dealing with the Kingdom traders as it makes him think fast. But if it rots within a few days, that is not going to work.

"Where are you heading anyway?"

"To Ur."

"Aah. Great place. Make sure you visit the temple in the morning and *Dancing Girl* in the evening."

"Dancing Girl?"

"Yes, she is famous—she comes from a mythical valley. You will find out when you get there."

The phrase used by the worker evokes an uneasy sensation in Ramey's mind. Why should the words dancing girl have any meaning for him—especially a girl in Sumer. He hurriedly packs his things up and makes his way to the dock.

The loading of the seafaring *dhow* takes some time. The chief of the crew, or as they called him, *Kaptan*, is particular about achieving a load balance in the boat. He makes sure the foredeck is one half of the load in the aft, but not any less. He does not want the boat's nose pointing down, but he also does not want it to lift too much. He checks the load distribution in relation to the main sails. He spends a good part of the morning shifting and re-shifting the cargo and passengers, mostly to achieve peace of mind for himself rather than to actually achieve any mystical load balance.

Ramey is standing on the dock, drenched in sweat and itchy around his neck from the salty, humid air and heat. As he is about to board, he thinks he sees Dogar among the passengers who have already boarded. He is not sure he wants to be on the same boat with him. If he stays behind, he will have to wait for the next *dhow* going west, which might not be for a few days, and he does not want to sit around in this port. He takes a deep breath and steps on board. With three encounters within two weeks, his initial anger with Dogar has transformed from awkwardness to tolerance.

When Dogar sees him, he looks equally surprised. During their meeting in Mohenjo-Daro neither had spoken about their specific travel plans. Finally, the *dhow* is underway. Ramey is thankful for the breeze on the open ocean that makes the humidity bearable. He also gets to experience the power and versatility of the triangular lateen sails. But he cannot understand the actual functioning of the rigging—the lateen sails and the long yard mounted on the main mast—and the constant shifting, adjusting, and occasional unfurling and furling. But he learns to keep his head down when the *Kaptan* gives an order for the yard to be swung around. The first couple of times he is caught unawares, and would have been hit, if not for the alertness of a passenger sitting next to him, who pushes him down to his knees. After that Ramey shifts his seat and ends up sitting only a couple of seats away from Dogar. There is almost nowhere on the boat where he can be completely safe from the effects of the sail operations. There are a couple of places where the rotating masts do not reach, but that is where coiled ropes are stored, and when needed, let out very rapidly. Getting his foot caught in an unspooling coil would be worse than being hit by a mast on the head.

No one can tell Ramey how long it is going to take to reach their destination of the holy city of Ur.

"Depends on the winds," people say.

"What depends upon the wind?"

"Our speed."

Ramey looks at the swirling sails and the white-caps on the ocean. "Well, we have plenty of wind."

"Depends upon the direction of the wind."

"The wind seems to be pushing us in the right direction. Is that good?"

"Yes, but it depends upon the changes in the speed and direction of the wind, and whether there are gusts and swirls in it."

Ramey realizes no one really knows and sits back in his seat.

In the river he can count on a current that always flows in one direction—downriver. And a current speed that varies only with the seasons—swift during the monsoons and slow during the dead of winter. Yes, there are eddies and whirlpools, backwaters behind midstream islands, shallows and sandbars, but most of the time they can be anticipated and maneuvered around. What counts is the effort by the rowers. This business of having to harness and depend on a fickle propulsion system of wind seems much more of a gamble. Add to that the unpredictability of the waves, the swells, the storms, and the vastness of the ocean. Ramey begrudgingly realizes it requires a much greater level of skill and experience to travel even a short distance on the ocean. He promises himself that if his *dhow* runs aground on a sand bar, he will not volunteer to jump into the water to help push the boat off. The *Kaptan* will just have to use the wind, the sails and oars to coax the boat off the shallows.

Voyage to the Empire

The heaving and swaying of the river boats has never bothered Ramey, so he believes he has a strong stomach. But the motion in the sea is much more complex, and nearly gets the better of him. Sitting two seats away, Dogar notices the distress in Ramey's face and passes him a slice of lemon. Sucking on the lemon settles Ramey's stomach and gives him time to adjust to the small wave impacts. Before long he adjusts to the pace of sea travel and recognizes this is a voyage not just a trip. There is plenty of time to talk to the other passengers, as they will share each other's company for an extended period. He also finds it a good opportunity to learn more about his destination.

He thanks Dogar for the slice of lemon and makes an effort at small talk, "I did not expect to see you. What takes you to Sumer?"

"My travel plans are somewhat irregular. Sometimes news about opportunities reaches me and I must leave urgently. This is one of those trips."

"I don't see your helper with you, or a bundle of fabric."

Dogar laughs, "My business with the empire is mostly in metals—that is what takes me there. They have an insatiable appetite for metals with their need for weapons, statues and decorative panels for palace and temple doors."

Ramey listens half-heartedly. Dogar is carrying samples of ores and refined metals. He has always been in sales and has adapted himself to selling these metals rather than cloth.

Glancing at Dogar in the bright sun, Ramey sees deep creases not there three years ago. This man has obviously been through a lot, but Ramey feels no sympathy for him. He has brought it on himself and caused grief for others.

After a while Dogar addresses him again. "First time, you say?"

"Yes." He already told that to Dogar at his house.

"You are probably carrying some *cowrie shells* as currency."

"Yes." Ramey can't figure out how Dogar knows he is carrying a small bag of them.

Ramey has already used them to buy food and to pay for his overnight stay beyond. He hopes they will sustain him in the kingdom until he is able to sell some jewelery.

"*Cowrie shells* won't work there. And stop saying kingdom. Tell people you are going to Sumer."

"Sumer?"

"People between the two rivers say, 'We are from Sumer.'"

"They don't use *cowrie shells*?"

Cowrie Shells

"Not for day to day. First go to the money changer and change *cowrie shells* to *shekels*."

"*Shekels*?"

"Yes." Dogar pulls out a bronze coin from his bag.

Ramey begins to feel at ease with Dogar. "Can I see your metal?'

"You mean the *shekel*? Here, why?"

Ramey rubs the coin between his fingers. "I overheard two men talking about *shekels* of barley." He points to the other side of the boat.

Dogar smiles, "You heard right. They are talking about the barley weight they can buy for one *shekel*. If the harvest is good, more barley. From town to town, one *shekel* of barley will vary."

Ramey rubs the coin one more time and hands it back to Dogar.

"Barley weight for one *shekel* changes every year and from place to place."

Dogar smiles at the innocent remark, "Now you know what a *shekel* is."

Ramey remembers the year of the big floods, when grain could not be had for any price. And the

Bronze Shekels

year the cotton harvest was nearly double the usual, and a few months later cloth was so plentiful that one could not trade it for much of anything.

Based on what Ramey has heard, he gives his destination as Ur, although he is not sure if it is a large enough or affluent enough place for his products.

"You will probably have to go to Babylon or even Nineveh," Dogar tells him, "But you may want to spend a few days in Ur to become familiar with the ways of Sumer. Ur is a holy place with the most revered temple. The temple is revered because it is old, not because it is an impressive structure. And the king leaves it to the priests to run realizing he cannot collect taxes from the priests. This way, as long as he keeps his hands off, he does not have to spend much money for the temple."

"What are taxes and why does the king want them?"

Dogar laughs out loud. Ramey blushes and curses himself under his breath.

"I apologize," Dogar says. "The king collects a portion of each person's wealth at the end of each year."

"Hmm."

"And the part he takes away is called tax. The more wealth you have, the more he takes from you."

"Why?"

"He needs money to build palaces and roads—and to pay the soldiers."

"What if you don't pay?"

"Very simple. The king will send soldiers who will take the money from you by force."

"What if I stop the soldiers?"

Dogar drops his voice to a whisper, "If you are lucky, you will be taken away and locked up in prison. If you are unlucky, you will be killed, your family will be made slaves, and all your wealth will be taken away."

Ramey looks around, "Why are you whispering?"

Dogar motions for Ramey to keep his voice down, "You never know who is listening."

Ramey sits back with a resigned look and whispers, "I think I get this. I pay the king so he can have soldiers. And he uses soldiers to take my money, right?"

"Well, that is not all that the soldiers do. They also protect you from other soldiers sent by other kings."

"Someday you will have to tell me why any other king will send soldiers. This is enough lesson for one day—it has given me a headache."

Dogar settles back in his seat.

Ramey cannot separate Zara's memory from Dogar's presence. That is the most painful part of having Dogar as his guide.

The voyage in the *dhow* continues for three days with stops at overnight inns where Ramey tastes unfamiliar food and needs the green drink in the morning to fight back the heat and salty humidity of the sea. By now he has heard of the green beans being referred to as coffee.

On the last day Dogar seeks Ramey out. "I want to again apologize about my behavior towards you three years back."

"Please," Ramey holds up his hand, "You have already told me of your regret. Don't mention it again—it brings back painful memories."

Dogar pauses, "I remember you telling me about the secret of drilling hard gemstones."

"Yes, what about it?"

"I don't know about it, but I can foresee you will be asked about it. The authorities in Sumer extract and collect useful information from everyone. They want Sumer to be the largest and strongest empire. They know about the Egyptians who they think are too involved in religion and matters of the next world. They are envious of their construction, but Sumer does not have the hard rock that Egypt has."

"I am not sure who the Egyptians are, but they must be somewhere far away. Are they the only other big empire?"

"The Sumerians have also heard of the Chinese, but think of them as provincial, so not much of a rival. They send spies everywhere to learn from those who are more advanced."

"The Sumerians have never come to the Indus Valley."

"They must have, but we in the Indus Valley are too primitive for them. This drilling technique of yours might awaken them."

"We are not that primitive."

"Well, be prepared to be asked how you drill through a hard gemstone with a soft metal drill."

"They can ask all they want, but I am not going to tell."

Dogar shakes his head, "In that case, there may be some difficulties."

The Secrets of the Jewelers

The next morning. they arrive in Ur where Dogar leaves the boat and goes his separate way. Ramey tags along with some other travelers who go first to drop their luggage at an inn, and then to the temple to give offerings. They light the incense sticks, throw some myrrh in the holy fire, and ask the priest to bless their journey, which costs them one *shekel* each. Ramey is glad he took Dogar's suggestion and changed some of his *cowrie shells* for *shekels* though he is surprised how little they fetch. He was told the barley harvest was not good this year, so the *shekels* are up in value. He cannot understand why his *cowrie shells* did not also go up in value. He understands the value of making an offering to the gods. He has always done that in Harappa, but it does not involve any priests or temples. He would get up at sunrise, wash up, and facing the sun, make his offerings to the Goddess, ending with giving some food to the birds and insects.

Sumerian Temple of Ur

After resting at the inn for a couple of days to get over his travel fatigue, Ramey takes the jewelry he brought to sell and goes to visit the market-place. He wants to assess the level of goods being traded at the various stores. His pieces are so rare he does not want to cheapen their value by showing them to people who do not know about precious gemstones. He first looks at the shops around the temple that carry items for the pilgrims, but they seem to be selling mostly cheap trinkets. Apparently even cheap trinkets are made valuable by their proximity to the temple grounds, especially if a priest has blessed them. Pilgrims buy these to take back as holy objects,

Further from the temple, Ramey finds one jeweler who is selling high quality ornaments, so he enters the store.

"You have some very fine jewelry."

"Thank you. What would you like to see?"

Ramey points to the display counter. "The turquoise in the back."

"Good choice. This is a very lucky stone."

Ramey decides to check if the man is a jeweler or merely a salesman.

"Is that right? How do you shape it? Is it along the crystal cleavage?"

"Hmm. Cleavage, yes, yes, that is how it is done."

Ramey knows turquoise is not split along cleavage but shaped along the lines of hardness. This man is merely a salesman.

While chatting some more, Ramey learns about the business and trade of jewelry making and notices a stern looking man hovering by the store close enough to overhear what they are talking about. The next time he wanders by, he motions to the owner to come to him, who then leaves Ramey and walks over to the stranger. While the two of them whisper to each other, Ramey has a chance to take a good look at the man. His hooked nose stands out to Ramey. He has seen this facial characteristic in other Sumerians, but the nose on this man's face is more prominent.

After a few moments, the store owner returns. Ramey waits for an explanation or excuse for the absence, but he resumes their conversation as if nothing has happened. All through their discussion, as Ramey supplies information about the process of turning gems into jewelry, he also tries to sense what value is being placed on the skill employed by the craftsmen. Gradually Ramey learns that though not very knowledgeable about the jewelry making techniques, this jeweler does have an eye for the skill employed. It remains to be seen what kind of value the Ur bazaar will put on what Ramey has brought from the Indus Valley. This store is as good a place as any to see.

He first takes out the white-fired steatite beads, progressing to the glazed steatite, including some with the bluish-gold hue. The store owner expresses appropriate interest but keeps his admiration in check until he has seen Ramey's ultimate offering.

It takes Ramey the good part of an hour, but he finally takes out a necklace made with the gold-streaked, deep blue lapis beads. This masterpiece has a 7 centimeter long bead at the center. He glances at the widening eyes of the jeweler, waiting for him to exhale, but the jeweler maintains an expression of admiration and an affirmation of the value of the piece.

"That is a remarkable piece. But tell me, what gemstone is this?"

"It is called lapis lazuli."

"Do you have a piece of the raw stone not yet turned into a bead?"

"Yes." Ramey hands him a small chunk. The store owner reaches under his counter and takes out a well-worn small slab of stone. He places the piece of lapis next to the slab.

"May I?" he asks as he looks at Ramey. He holds the lapis fragment and draws a scratch across his stone slab, incising a clear straight line showing the lapis is harder than the stone slab. Next, he takes out a small bronze nail with a sharp point and tries to scratch the lapis with it, again looking at Ramey before trying it. The bronze nail does not even scratch the lapis.

"This is a very hard gemstone."

"Yes, it is." Ramey smiles.

The shop owner looks surprised, "The bronze nail cannot scratch it, yet your gemstone can easily scratch my stone slab of calcite."

"Yes, I see that." The smile remains on Ramey's face.

Ancient Hand Drill and Bronze-age Necklace

"You know what I am thinking, but do you want me to actually say it?"

"Go ahead."

"Alright. How did you drill a hole through it? The bronze is not hard enough."

Ramey's smile now turns to a serious expression. "We have developed a way to do it."

"I am sure you have because I am looking at the result of your work. But how? Tell me."

Ramey shakes his head, "I am sorry—I cannot."

The store owner shifts in his seat and changes his approach,

"So where did you say you were from? Some river valley?"

"The Indus Valley," Ramey answers, "you have never heard of it? Indus Valley is very well known." A smile escapes the jeweler's lips at the hubris of this traveler from one of the less-developed societies, while standing in Sumer—and especially in holy Ur.

"I may have," he says with a wave of his hand. "What was the last big war you Indus people fought?"

"War?"

"Yes war. Or battle. Tell me the name of a famous one that may jog my memory about where you come from?"

Ramey doesn't understand the question. "Are you talking of fighting? Killing people?"

"Yes, yes. So how many have you killed?"

Ramey hesitates, "Nobody. Why would I kill someone?"

The jeweler looks at him oddly, "To win honors, of course. How do your people win honors?"

"By helping other people."

The jeweler realizes the pointlessness of this conversation, but makes one last attempt,

"Well, in that case, I have never heard of Indus. But who is your king? Maybe he is famous?"

"King? One man who would rule over all others? We don't do that. All people in Indus are equal."

The jeweler can't believe his ignorance.

"So, your people live in caves?"

"Caves? No, we live in brick houses. We have fresh running water coming to our houses every day. Every house has a toilet and a drain to take the waste out. The trash in the streets is taken away every day. Our streets are not dirty like the streets in Ur."

"You are describing how you will live when you go to paradise after dying. I am asking you of this life." The jeweler knows that even the nobility's houses in Sumer do not have fresh flowing water and toilets with drains. This is some deluded man who is describing something he saw in a dream. He probably lives in a hovel, and drinks from a stale pond used by cattle and horses. The trash the jeweler has thrown behind his own house last week, or last month, is still there. So, trash removal is another fantasy of this clumsy villager.

The jeweler goes back to a more productive topic. "So how do you drill a hole through a hard gemstone with a bronze drill?"

"My uncle developed this technique. It is a secret."

Ramey is worried he is going to lose the sale. As a precaution, he keeps a light grip on one end of the string that is woven through the beads. Everything from the steatites to lapis is spread out on a brilliant white cloth of soft cotton that covers the appraisal counter.

While his gems are being evaluated, a group of pilgrims stops by including a young woman wearing a dozen bangles on one arm and holding a rose. The jeweler just glances at them. He knows pilgrims are only looking for cheap trinkets. While looking around the store, the girl shakes her arm. Ramey, who senses the fragrance of a fresh rose near him, is so distracted by the sonorous jangle that he completely loses concentration. For a few moments he does not know where he is. It takes tremendous effort to regain his composure and realize he is still in the jewelry store in Ur. After a couple of attempts to understand the cause of his distraction, he gives up and tries to focus on the task at hand.

Seeing no holy trinkets in the shape of the temple building or statues of gods, the pilgrims leave. The jeweler barely twitches a muscle for these onlookers and gets back to fingering beads and necklaces brought by Ramey. After some thought, he offers a sum for Ramey's whole stock.

Ramey just sits there, seemingly considering the purchase offer from the jeweler. But still shaken from the incident, he is incapable of making a rational decision at this moment. He gathers up his wares, promising to return the next day. The jeweler wonders if he is going to walk around in order to seek a better price. Ramey has no intention of repeating something that took him a good part of the morning. He does not believe he can strike a better bargain. At the last minute, the jeweler raises his offer, but Ramey feigns an appointment with his friend he cannot miss and leaves. He reaches his inn lost in his bewilderment, goes to his room and lies down exhausted. It is there he starts to discover a passage to his heart that leads him to the memory of Zara—a memory he had buried, suddenly unearthed in this distant land.

CHAPTER 9

Symbols That Speak

The next morning, Ramey is received with a warm welcome by the jeweler.. The overnight cooling off period has given them both time to think things over. The jeweler has realized the rarity of the long, gold-streaked lapis lazuli beads, and has even thought of a wealthy customer who visits Ur for his annual pilgrimage from Nineveh, and who always buys rare, expensive gifts for his newest mistress. Ramey also has had time to think. He has spoken with a couple of guests at the inn about the market conditions and is satisfied he is getting as good a deal as any Outworlder could get. While concluding his trade, he decides to inquire about the hook-nosed man.

"Who was the hawk eyeing us yesterday?"

"Hawk?"

Ramey grabs his nose and tries to stretch and bend it downward.

The jeweler bursts out laughing, "Are you making fun of our elegant noses? What about that fat one on your face?"

"This one is beautiful," Ramey says as he touches his nose.

"His name is Arkan, or at least that is what he tells me. He is a minder." Ramey's face is a blank. The jeweler lowers his voice to a whisper. "An informer for the king. I would advise you not to make many enquiries about anyone like that hawk. Watch what you say when one of them is near you—best to watch out all the time."

Arkan

Ramey recalls that in Mohenjo-Daro, Dogar warned him about the spies in Ur. He decides to be careful. As he is about to leave, he sees the jeweler grab a small pot covered with a lid from behind his seat. He reaches in and brings out a pat of damp clay. Ramey smells an odor like that in a potter's workshop. The jeweler puts the clay on a small wooden board and flattens it down. He takes out a stylus trimmed out of a reed and repeatedly presses its end into the clay, creating several small indentations. The variety, complexity, and sheer number of marks baffles Ramey.

"Those are a lot of symbols," he comments.

The jeweler lifts his head quizzically, looks at Ramey, and goes back to the pat of clay and the stylus. Ramey waits until the task is finished.

"Yes?" The jeweler lifts his head, wondering why this foreigner is still standing there. "What did you say?"

"Nothing," Ramey says at first, then continues. "What were you doing?"

"Recording our transaction."

"Recording?"

"Yes, you can't expect me to remember all the details of the transaction. I am buying a dozen different kinds of beads and necklaces from you for different prices. This way I have a record."

"But you were making some symbols."

"Yes, these symbols speak to me—they tell me my thoughts."

The store owner cannot believe he is having this conversation. He thought of Ramey as a skilled jewelry maker and a shrewd trader, but during the last few moments whatever high opinion he had formed of this Indus man dissolves each time Ramey opens his mouth. He regrets having offered him a large sum for his beads. He probably could have had them for half as much. He takes another deep breath, and with exasperation, or maybe it is pity, says with a sigh, "Yes?"

A Sumerian Cuneiform (right) — Indus Valley Seal (left)

"How do these symbols speak to you?" Ramey's words sound more like a plea than a question.

The jeweler looks down at the wet pat of clay and starts reading. "On this 11th day of the third month of the great god Nanna, I purchased from one Ramey, who claims to be Indus, the following items . . . Do you want me to read the list of what you brought with you, or do you still remember them?"

Ramey senses the change in the jeweler's attitude and is sorry he asked. He picks up his lightened bundle and starts to leave.

"I wanted to learn, but if this is your family secret, please forgive me."

The jeweler laughs out loud. Ramey is mortified.

"My simple friend, these symbols are not a secret, but I don't have the time or the skill to teach you the cuneiform script. If you want to know more, walk down to the next turn in this street and into the alley on your left where there is a row of scribes sitting on the side. Go to one of them, and for a couple of *shekels* he will gladly spend the day teaching you our script. I just assumed everyone who comes into Sumer can read this script."

Ramey thanks him and leaves. As he is walking away, he notices the hook-nosed man, Arkan, heading toward the store. He does not meet Ramey's gaze but keeps up his purposeful steps. Is it to learn what was sold or bought, or something else?

After walking for a while, Ramey reaches the first turn in the road and looks to his left. The entrance to the scribes' alley is partly covered with a tarp, apparently hung by a couple of the scribes near the entrance to protect them from the direct sun. He is about to enter the alley when he hears a voice on his right.

"Friend, friend, excuse me."

He turns his head and sees a man carrying a bundle on his shoulder, trying to get his attention. Ramey stops. The man puts the bundle down on the ground.

"You are from the Indus, aren't you?"

Ramey does not say anything, but the man greets him like a long-lost friend.

"Welcome, welcome. You are a pilgrim to Ur. Great, me too. See, I know the Indus talk."

Ramey smiles at this man's notion that if he interjects some words from the Indus Valley into the conversation, it becomes Indus talk.

"I have been here one week," the man says, "and now I am going home."

Ramey thinks as soon as the man stops to breathe, he will turn into the alley, but he is able to talk without inhaling and continues speaking.

"Surely you are from Monjo. I can tell. I have been to Monjo. It is my favorite town."

Ramey considers denying he is from any Monjo, but that would only prolong the encounter. Any attempt to correct Monjo to Mohenjo-Daro would do the same, so he simply resigns himself to listening, once glancing at the scribes' alley to make sure he is in the right place.

The man keeps talking, "I had a business transaction here, and I have concluded my business very successfully. The people I was helping were so pleased, they gave me six woolen shawls. Do you want to see one?"

Ramey shakes his head, but the man doesn't stop talking.

"I now find out a law they have here. I am only allowed to take five shawls with me. Imagine, I'll have to throw one shawl away. It is a pity. Can I give one to you?"

Ramey is amused by this novel sales approach. He recognizes the man as a fellow salesman. He wants to prolong this entertaining part of the conversation to practice the technique and use it in future. But he wants to get to the scribes' alley.

He starts to walk away when he notices the corner of a red woolen shawl peeking out of the man's bundle. His feet stop moving. He cannot understand why the red shawl has brought him to a standstill. The man is still talking, but Ramey cannot hear him. He remembers the moment when Zara extracted the promise of a red woolen shawl from him as the price of his journey to Sumer. Even though he has tried his best to forget Zara, and everything associated with her, perhaps his heart has kept the red shawl as a memento. Is this an omen? He was not even looking for a red shawl. The Goddess must have sent this fast-talking man trying to give him one. His heart sinks at the prospect of refusing a gift from the Goddess and incurring her wrath. If he buys this shawl, he will only be torturing himself with the memory of a long-lost love, now beyond his reach. If he refuses to take it and walks away, he will be the most ungrateful person in the eyes of the Goddess and will surely meet a terrible end. The shawl purchase will at least relieve this torment.

The shrewd vendor with a novel sales technique, packs one red woolen shawl tightly into a cloth bundle, and after some haggling, accepts four *shekels* for it. Ramey is no expert on shawls, but this one appears to be an exquisite specimen of high-quality wool, workmanship and color brilliance. A fleeting image of the beautiful Zara wrapped in this red shawl flashes in his mind, but he quickly suppresses it. There is no beautiful Zara in his life. He tries to think of his purchase as fulfillment of a command from the Goddess—not his promise to Zara who is no longer in his life. As Ramey starts to walk away toward the scribes' alley, he hears the shawl salesman address another passerby. "Friend, friend, you are from the western mountains, are you not?" This brings a smile to Ramey's lips.

A short distance into the alley, Ramey finds a scribe who is not busy.

"A receipt or a bill of sale?" he asks Ramey.

Ramey's expression is blank. He does not know what the scribe is asking, so he remains quiet.

"A petition to the king then, or a prayer for the temple?" As there is still no response, the scribe makes his last attempt, "What then, a message for *Dancing Girl*?" Still no response. The scribe becomes annoyed, "Do you have something you want me to do, or are you here to waste my time, and also yours?"

"I want to learn what you are doing," Ramey says respectfully.

"I am a scribe. I write things down for people. Where are you from?"

"The Indus Valley," Ramey says trying to appear confident.

"I think I have heard of the Indus Valley. There is a river there, yes."

Ramey wants to tell him the Indus is a mighty river, not like this muddy stream Euphrates the Sumerians call a river, but he lets it pass.

"Don't you write things down?" the scribe inquires.

"We have our family seals, like this." Ramey takes out a steatite seal with his family's emblem on it.

The scribe feels the white-fired soapstone seal and rubs one finger over its smooth surface and along the edges of the clearly incised symbols.

"Fine work. Must take a while to make one. What does it say?"

"Say? Nothing. This is my family seal. This is our symbol. We mark our work with it. It is not a message, nor a list of things. It brings blessings to our family."

"All right. And what do you want from me?"

"I want to learn your work."

"Do you want to become my apprentice for a year or two? There is no pay, but you don't have to pay me anything."

"No, I am hoping I can learn this afternoon."

The scribe laughs, "Well, this is Ur, a place of miracles, so who knows." He looks at Ramey's face and realizes the young man is serious. There are no other customers this morning, so why not.

"What brings you to town?"

"I am selling jewelry. Do you want to see some?"

"No, I don't want any jewelry. Have you finished your transaction? And have you made a record?"

"Record? No. What is the record for? I know what I have sold." Ramey points to his heart.

"Well, that is because it just happened. Yesterday? This morning? But will you remember it six months from now, or six years? Probably not. What I do will preserve the memory for not only six years, but sixty, or maybe even six hundred years. Do you want a record of the sale you made? You can take it back to your family and any family member will know all the details."

"How much?" Ramey asks.

"To make a record? Depending upon how long. A record is usually one half to one *shekel*." Seeing the uncertainty in Ramey's face, the scribe adds, "And that includes a lesson in writing also."

Ramey sits down. The scribe reaches under his compact floor desk and brings out a pat of moist clay, and then another one. The aroma hits Ramey's nostrils. The scribe takes out two reed pens and hands one to Ramey. He glances at Ramey's reed, exchanges it with his own, then takes out a bronze dagger and begins shaping the ends of the reeds into styluses. He flattens both pats of moist clay on a wooden board to a one-inch thickness and four inches square. He shows Ramey how to hold the reed stylus between his thumb and first two fingers. "Hold it firmly, but no need to apply so much pressure that your knuckles are strained. Now press the stylus into the clay like this." He incises a wedge-shaped indentation of 1/2 inch width and a similar depth.

When the clay sticks to Ramey's stylus, the scribe takes out a damp rag and hands it to him. "Clean up the end before incising again, and don't dig so deep."

Ramey timidly tries again, making a barely perceptible indentation. He wipes the end of the reed and tries to deepen the second wedge.

"Why don't you first watch what I am doing," the scribe says. "Tell me your name." Upon hearing the name, the scribe repeats it under his breath a couple of times and using his reed stylus makes half a dozen wedge-shaped marks in the clay.

"Which one is the symbol for my name?" Ramey asks.

"All of these are," the scribe answers and then sounds out what he has incised, "Ra-ha-may."

"Hmm, it sounds different."

"Of course, it will sound different. You are not Sumerian and Indus people don't have any writing. You can go to the temple and change your name to a good Sumerian name like Akkad, and I'll show you how to write it accurately."

"Akkad," Ramey rolls it around in his mouth. "Is that your name?"

The scribe grins. "So, what did you sell?"

Ramey hesitates. Should he tell this perfect stranger what is essentially a family matter? He starts going through the list of items he sold wondering if he is taking a risk in revealing his business transactions. He decides to get his doubt and suspicion out of his heart. "People tell you things. What if something is a secret?" The scribe looks puzzled.

The alley is a little busier now, as some of the temple-goers are stopping by to get their prayers inscribed, or at least their name and the name of some relative who is sick, and for whom they want the priests to pray. Others have concluded their business transactions and are there to get them recorded. Ramey occasionally glances at the passersby. Those with odd-looking clothing or facial features catch his eye. During one of these momentary pauses, he thinks he sees the hook-nosed man walk by, looking at them intently.

The scribe finally realizes what his customer is asking. He has been asked this question many times before. "We scribes adhere to a very strict code of silence. We do not divulge anything we learn while writing. Before we are allowed to offer our services, we must appear at the temple and go through an oath-taking ceremony. I manage to adhere to the code by simply forgetting everything you tell me. I forget what my customers tell me before they have reached the front door of their dwelling." Ramey is satisfied with this explanation.

The scribe hands the still moist clay to Ramey. "You must be staying at an inn. Take this to their kitchen and they will fire it for you." Seeing Ramey's skepticism, he continues, "It only needs light firing, the kitchen hearth can do that easily. The clay does not need to develop a glaze." As he is leaving the alley, Ramey sees the government spy Arkan walking toward the scribe's stall.

Ramey stops in the main marketplace to eat and sits for a while watching all the visitors who have come to Ur. It is evening by the time he reaches the inn. Upon entering he sees the innkeeper chatting with another customer.

"I would like to get this fired," Ramey says.

The innkeeper glances at the tablet that has dried out a bit by now. "Take it back to the kitchen, they will know what to do." He points to a door to the back. "You look pleased, you must have had a profitable day."

"Yes, yes."

"So where did you say you are from? Some river valley?"

"The Indus Valley," Ramey answers, "you have never heard of it? The Indus Valley is very well known."

The innkeeper shakes his head but a customer who is listening to this exchange speaks up.

"Tell me again, what was the name of your Valley?"

"The Indus Valley," Ramey says, hoping the man may have heard of it.

The customer turns to the innkeeper, "Doesn't that name sound familiar?"

The innkeeper has a blank expression, but the customer goes on, "Think of a few months back, in Pleasure Alley—you certainly knew the name of the Indus Valley then."

The innkeeper has a sheepish look on his face as he turns to Ramey, "Now I remember. Indus, the valley that is famous, not for kings or wars, but for dancing girls."

"So, the Indus Valley does exist. I thought she had made up the name," says the customer.

The innkeeper and the other customer laugh and exchange a hearty handshake. The innkeeper turns to do other work and the customer goes to his room, leaving Ramey standing there seething.

NIghttime, Pleasure Alley

He did not like these two men referring to his beloved homeland in such a derisive manner. But why is this impersonal joke or even insult making him so upset? Is it because everybody in Harappa once called Zara, *Dancing Girl,* after their Spring Festival? Surely there is no connection. Ramey leaves the clay tablet in the kitchen and goes to see the innkeeper again. He finds him alone.

Upon seeing Ramey, he grins, "I am glad you like our city."

Ramey lowers his voice, "I need your advice. I am a stranger here, unaccustomed to the laws and customs of Sumerians. I don't want to get into any trouble. May I ask if any minder has come around asking about me."

The innkeeper's expression turns serious. "I cannot answer that question. It will get *me* into trouble. However, I can advise you. It appears you are hiding the knowledge of your jewelry making methods from us, which is certainly your business. Yet you want to learn and take back what is of value in Sumer—our writing."

It is beginning to dawn on Ramey. So that is what the government minder Arkan is upset about. Ramey refused to tell the jeweler in the marketplace how it is possible to drill a hole through a very hard gemstone using a drill made of bronze, which is softer than the gem. His enquiries about the writing method in the scribe's alley have also drawn the spy's attention and made him a target. He thanks the innkeeper and goes to his room. Apparently, the Sumerians believe their cuneiform writing to be the greatest achievement of their civilization and a cornerstone of their empire.

Cuneiform is the only system with true alphabets and the Sumerians do not want other people to steal it from them, least of all people who do not want to share their own knowledge. Ramey decides it best to stop enquiring about the Sumerian kingdom and how it functions.

CHAPTER 10

Pleasure Alley

The evening meal at the inn is served early. The aroma of cooking from the kitchen fills Ramey's nostrils. What is this fascination the Sumerians have with lamb's meat? The smell of burning fat the Sumerians crave revolts Ramey. Why can't they eat goat meat like in the Indus Valley? He has tried to tell the kitchen staff at the inn, but they merely laugh at him and say it is goat meat that stinks. He is sure they are making it up to annoy him.

At the table Ramey sits next to a visitor from Babylon who has come to make offerings at the ancient, holy temple of Ur. After the meal the man asks Ramey if he wants to come along with him for a stroll. Together, they walk out onto the main road, and pass through the central market.

Soon they turn into an alley that is a little too lively for this time of the evening. The sound of music filters out from behind closed doors—inside the rooms are lit up. Ramey's senses are treated to a

Illuminations, Pleasure Alley

fragrance of perfume and incense emanating from each doorway.

"This is Ur's famous Pleasure Alley. Pilgrims who come to Ur to offer devotions at the Holy Temple in the morning, come down here at night." Ramey looks perplexed, and the other man laughs, "This street is for the business of the night."

"What is the business of the night?"

"Don't you lie with women at night?"

"Oh," Ramey says. In addition to music, he hears loud conversations behind one of the doors. The inside appears crowded.

"That loud place is where I saw the famous *Dancing Girl* when I was here last time."

"*Dancing Girl?*"

"Yes. She comes from some valley. But the dance is only the first dish. After that she is available for an extra payment. Usually there is a line of men waiting."

"Oh. . ."

"Go and find out if she still works there. She keeps moving around. But be careful—people say she casts a spell, so the men are always coming back for her."

Most of the doorways are shut, but small windows are open through which lights, colorful drapes and glimpses of clothing are visible. Ramey is amazed at the size and scale of Pleasure Alley. In Harappa, a town a third of the size of this holy city of Ur, he knows of only two or three women reputed to be available to men for an hour or so in exchange for cash, clothing or a supply of food. Two of these women are young widows who originally came from smaller settlements some distance away and have no other family connections in town. One woman got into the business when quite young, much to her family's chagrin and shame. What these women do is considered a social aberration. But here in the holy city of Ur, in a society where such acts are considered immoral and illegal, to find a whole alley devoted to the business astonishes him.

"So now do you understand what Pleasure Alley refers to?" Ramey's companion asks. Ramey is no longer surprised. They come to a doorway which is rather quiet and his companion points to it.

"Let us go into this one," he says, but sees the hesitation on his face. "Well, you can come inside and just wait for me."

Ramey follows him into a waiting room. Four men are playing a board game while two others are chatting. A man standing on one side of the room gestures to them and greets Ramey's companion in a low voice. They sit down on two low seats and lean against the wall. At the far end of the room hangs a translucent drape, behind which Ramey can see a man and a woman on a low bed in a dimly lit area. The man is moving on top of the woman: each of his moves elicits a low moan from the woman. This scene continues until the man lets out a sound between a sigh and a yell, and collapses. A few moments later he gets up, but the woman stays lying on the bed. The man who had initially greeted them motions to one of the waiting men, who gets up and goes behind the drape. It does not take him long before he begins his actions, accompanied by the woman's moans in a slightly different tone, as if adjusting to this man's weight, size and vigor.

Ramey turns to his companion with an expression that seems to say, "Is this what it is about?" If the translucent curtain is meant to increase attraction, it has the opposite effect on Ramey. "I am going to get some fresh air," he says and gets up to leave.

"If you are looking for a better house, you won't find it. This one has the most class."

Ramey waves at him and walks out. The alley is busier now. Small groups of men are heading towards specific houses, while others are taking a leisurely stroll, as if window shopping. Men occasionally stop and peek in through a door, or enter, glance around, and then come back out.

Shadowy Figures in Pleasure Alley

Ramey has gone half-way down the alley when he stops abruptly. Up ahead, four or five shops away, in the glimmer of the lamps, he notices Dogar. He has not seen or heard from him since their arrival in Ur and assumed he had gone on to Babylon. So, to see him still in Ur and in this street, startles him. Dogar is much older than the other customers in the alley. Although respectably dressed, he looks disheveled and does not seem aware of his appearance.

Dogar tries to enter one shop and is rudely pushed out. A couple of shops later, the scene is repeated. This is unusual, because the attendants who stand at the doors are trying to entice men to come in, not push them rudely away. The third time it happens, the attendant rebukes Dogar loudly and Ramey catches the words. "Move on, move on, she is no longer here." Dogar does not seem to understand. With an expression of urgency, bordering on pitiful, he tries to say something to the attendant, but Ramey cannot hear the words. The attendant finally gives him a shove and Dogar is forced to move on. The attendant remains outside to make sure he does not come back.

Dogar keeps walking and soon leaves the alley. Ramey wonders what Dogar was talking about, so he walks up to the attendant. Seeing a young man who is clearly from out of town, he greets him with friendly words.

"Come on in, we have very nice girls."

Ramey smiles, "What was going on with that man?"

It takes the attendant a couple of moments to understand what Ramey is asking. He shakes his head, "Oh, it is a sad story—he has lost his senses."

"What do you mean? How?"

The guard looks at Ramey wondering if he should waste his time on him. Reassuring himself that Ramey is young and from out of town, and a potential customer, he decides to indulge him for a few moments.

"I hear this man is a respectable businessman in his country. But when he is here in Ur, he is overcome with grief and loses his mind."

"What was he asking you?"

"He wants to know if his daughter is living here. He is convinced his daughter works in this alley and he has been trying to rescue her. He shows up every few months and each time turns into a lunatic when he enters the alley."

"Is she working here?"

"I don't even know who she is, but I have heard she is very beautiful and is known as *Dancing Girl*. She claims to have come from some mythical valley and spins tales of abundance, cleanliness, fresh running water and other lies no one believes. She has obviously made this place up in her head. No one has seen her in a couple of months. Maybe she has gone on to Babylon for the festival."

"But what is the story behind all this?" The attendant looks around but seeing no other prospective customers, he decides to continue the conversation.

"All this happened somewhere far away, so there are many versions. Apparently, she was seeing a very eligible young man and wanted to marry him. However, the gods must have cursed this crazy man, because in his haughtiness, he decided his daughter could do better. The girl's lover was extremely disappointed. The daughter was distraught and tried to poison herself, but they were able to give her an antidote. She survived but became dejected."

"What happened to the young man?"

"They say he hanged himself. But all this happened somewhere far away from Ur. This trader brought her here, rented a house, and began taking her to the temple every day, hoping that would cure her sadness, but to no avail. While conducting his business he would leave her by herself in the house. A beautiful young girl, alone and in a desperate state of mind, she became prey for unscrupulous men. A no-good ruffian enticed her to elope with him. The father searched and searched but could not find her—because she did not want to be found."

"Why would she not want to be found?"

"Some people say she eloped just to get even with him."

"Then what happened?"

"This hooligan kept her for a while, then passed her on to someone else, and she kept going from man to man. The father agreed to any demand the daughter made, and she made many, but she could not be straightened out. In time, she started dancing and working in one of these houses."

"Does she still work on this street?"

"Who knows? Now this man goes around, trying to find her, but she is always one step ahead of him, and keeps changing her location. Occasionally, she escapes to Babylon or Nineveh, and he loses her trail." The attendant suddenly remembers what he is supposed to be doing. "Come inside, we have a couple of nice girls," he adds with a laugh, "Just not his daughter."

Ramey thanks him, promises to come back, and moves on down the street. With a heavy heart, he looks for but never finds Dogar. The beautiful Zara, whom he once adored and wanted to marry, has come to this. This is all her father's doing. If he had not prevented their marriage, she could have lived a full and happy life with Ramey, even helping him in gem selection and jewelry design.

He can no longer smell the perfumes and the incense, only the stench of trash that permeates the air. He picks up his step and leaves the alley, returning to the inn. It takes him a long time to fall asleep.

CHAPTER 11

A Cry for Help

The next day is Ramey's last in Ur. He eats an early breakfast but misses the hot liquid made with green beans. He wonders if that is why the residents of Ur are not up early. He goes to the temple to make a final offering of gratitude before returning. After lighting the incense and making the monetary contribution, he is about to leave when he thinks he hears Dogar's voice and looks around. The voice is coming through an open door from a small chamber on one side of the altar. Engrossed in a serious conversation with one of the priests, he is certain it is indeed Zara's father. Ramey lingers but can barely make out the words.

"Your worship, you can help her. You have helped other women find the straight path."

"Those women wanted to be helped. She does not."

"She also wants to be helped now—finally. She can stay with you and become a votary of Nanna, the moon god."

The priest shakes his head. "No, no. No good can come of it. We have given her a chance before, twice, but she changes her mind and runs away. In fact, the last time she convinced two other devotees of Nanna to go with her. Her presence here has not been a good influence for the temple."

The main chamber of the temple where he is standing is now filled with a heavy scent of incense. Many devotee visitors have come early to make their offerings to begin their journeys home.

"But your worship, what else can I do?"

"Her coming here again is not good. Her presence in the temple was attracting the wrong kind of men."

Without saying anything, Dogar keeps staring at the priest like a man who has lost his way and does not know where go.

"You must take her with you."

"But your worship, you don't know about the Indus Valley. It is a simple place—a community of artisans and farmers. We don't have temples and learned people like you."

The priest rises. "Fine, fine. If the Indus is calm compared to Sumer, so much the better. The lack of priests and temples is no reason to leave her here, we have not been able to do anything for her."

Ramey has a bitter taste in his mouth and wants to slip away unseen, but his step is leaden, along with his heavy and grieved heart. The small delay in his departure is enough for Dogar to spot him. At first Dogar does not seem to recognize him, but then he composes himself, and tries to speak to Ramey. He has cleaned himself up, so he does not look so disheveled, but his face looks wan and drawn and his eyes are bleary. Compared to the cheerful, confident man Ramey met in Mohenjo-Daro, Dogar is a faded image of his former self.

When Ramey realizes Dogar is not averse to communicating with him, he takes a couple of steps towards him. Just then, Dogar loses his balance, as if from physical and mental exhaustion. Ramey grabs him, preventing him from collapsing to the ground, and asks one of the temple attendants for some water. A few sips help to revive Dogar. He looks gratefully at Ramey, "Thank you."

"I think you need to rest. Have you eaten anything?"

Dogar feebly shakes his head, so Ramey helps him walk out of the temple to one of the food stalls along the street. Ramey is nauseated by the smell of cooked lamb so early in the day, but he realizes Dogar needs it to restore his strength.

After a few bites of meat, Dogar appears a little steadier. Ramey does not want to talk about Zara or Pleasure Alley, or what he has overheard from the priest. He sits quietly, thinking of going to the inn to pack up and find transportation back to the Indus Valley. As he gets up, Dogar grabs his arm, and Ramey sees the look of a supplicant on Dogar's face. He is clearly seeking help but does not know how to ask.

"Ramey," his voice fades but he keeps holding on to Ramey's arm. Ramey sits down and waits for Dogar to catch his breath. The look on Dogar's face is a mix of shame and helplessness. He does not want to ask Ramey for anything but has no one else to turn to. Finally, he speaks.

"Ramey, I have found her." He does not say who he is talking about, and Ramey does not need to ask. "They were telling me she has gone to Babylon, but she is right here."

Ramey is not sure how to take all this in, but he is sure he cannot hear much more. He has spent the last three years trying to forget about Dogar, and to erase Zara and her memory from his consciousness. Now, in a matter of minutes, it all comes rushing back. A mix of pity and hate toward this man swirls in his thoughts. He wants to get up and tell him he does not want to hear about his troubles or those of his daughter. Neither of them exists for him.

"I am going to see her and take her with me," he says.

Ramey hears him but does not know how to respond. He cannot sort through his complex emotions. Dogar is feeling better, and a faint smile skims his face, but he is still physically weak and emotionally distraught. Ramey returns Dogar's smile. Now he should be able to leave and go about his business.

"Are you going to be all right? You look much better."

Dogar nods, so Ramey turns to go but Dogar stops him.

"Ramey, can you help me?"

"Do you want some money?"

"No, no," Dogar shakes his head, "I need help to rescue her."

What kind of help is he talking about? If Dogar is unable to say her name, then Ramey can also pose his question without using Zara's name. Is he planning to take her back forcibly? After what he heard from the priest, that approach is not likely to succeed.

"Does she want to leave?" Ramey does not think forcible removal is possible considering that Dogar has not succeeded previously.

"She is exhausted, weak, and not quite in her senses, but she does want to leave—I think."

He thinks? What does that mean? But if she truly doesn't want to leave, then what kind of help could Ramey offer?

"She is not well, so I need your help in supporting her to walk to the inn where I am staying, and then later onto the boat."

Surely Dogar remembers how he treated him three years ago. And now this request? Where is this man's self-respect and his sense of dignity? When he looks into Dogar's eyes, he realizes this man has no pride left after what his daughter has been doing. The daughter for whom Ramey was not considered good enough has been available to anyone for a couple of *shekels*, and from what Ramey has heard, sometimes even without any payment. And from what he understands, the first man with whom she eloped fed her a potion made from mind-altering herbs, so she lost the power of reason, and has simply became an instrument for satisfying desires—hers or anyone else's.

"Do you want me to go with you?"

"Yes, yes."

Ramey is sitting across from Dogar. The early worshippers have left the temple and the market area is getting busy. He can see people hurrying about trying to accomplish their chosen tasks, or simply going about their daily routines. His mind mirrors the to-and-fro motion of feet and bodies that he sees. He thinks of simply getting up and leaving, not sure he can deal with all the old memories and thoughts and attachments. Why does he owe this man anything other than he is also from the Indus Valley. And what is the exact nature of his relationship with his daughter? He finds it too painful to even think about.

Ramey has invested so much emotional energy trying to bury his past love deep down in his mind and in his heart. The partial sense of calm that has taken years to achieve is shattering.

CHAPTER 12

The Rescue

Ramey waits at the eating stall near the temple until Dogar can summon some strength. He feels squeamish about what might come next. He has already seen enough of the seamy side of Ur and does not think he can take any more. But as his mind drifts to thoughts of Zara, he cannot help but dwell on his past love for her. He feels the old bonds rising in his consciousness, but it is no longer a passionate love. Still, there are inescapable traces of affection and sympathy, and slowly, an increasing desire to help. And a strange sense of curiosity.

It takes Dogar nearly an hour, but the food, fresh air, and Ramey's presence help him regain enough physical stamina and measure of emotional calm, that he can stand up and walk. He motions to Ramey.

"Let's go and get it done."

Ramey's heart rises into his throat upon hearing the challenging way that Dogar describes what is to come. As they begin walking, Dogar's steps are brisk. A sense of purpose has given him energy, but Ramey hopes it is not his company that is making him so resolute. He is not planning to take the lead in the affair that may unfold. He is going along thinking of himself as a bystander rather than a participant.

Dogar is familiar with the streets and alleys of Ur. He has been making regular trips for selling the ores from the mountains, and many journeys in search of his daughter. After walking for half an hour, Ramey notices the character of the neighborhood begin to change. The area looks poorer than the rest of town and neglected. Only the main thoroughfares and the vicinity of the temple are swept regularly, while the trash is left to rot in alleys like this neighborhood.

"Are we lost?" Ramey asks. "Do you know the way?"

Dogar does not answer, but keeps walking with a reassuringly confident step, and turns into a small alley. Seeing the backs of a couple of buildings to one side, Ramey realizes they are close to Pleasure Alley, but behind it with no apparent access. They would have to go a long way around to get there, but it is possible some of the establishments have back doors. The back side of Pleasure Alley is drab, blending into the desert earth. The walls, floors, streets, and doorways have all gathered a coating of powdery earth turning them into a nondescript, depressing beige. Pleasure Alley itself is a festival of color and sound, bright and flashy, with beads and garments draped over walls, and visible portions of buildings painted in bright, garish colors. Ramey's surroundings are the opposite of Pleasure Alley. It is eerily muted and silent.

Finally, Dogar stops in the middle of an intersection of three alleys and looks around as if trying to jog his memory. "I have seen this area only at night, so give me a minute," he says.

Ramey is not eager to enter any of these buildings. If Dogar cannot remember the exact shop, it is fine with Ramey. He will return to the inn and pack up his belongings.

Dogar does not say anything, he just stands there squinting, shading his eyes, and slowly turning around, examining each place, visualizing how it might have appeared at night. Finally, he steps towards a door and knocks. There is no answer, so he pushes it in and motions to Ramey to follow. They enter a courtyard surrounded by rooms on three sides, with the door left ajar. A couple of other doors are wide open. The rooms are unoccupied with an unmade bed and a few abandoned belongings in each. Ramey stands in the middle of the courtyard glancing around, as Dogar disappears into one of the rooms. After some time, Ramey's earlier thought of bolting the scene enters his mind, but he resists the urge. He does not want to leave without telling Dogar. Finally, the door creaks open and Dogar comes out, supporting a slight figure wrapped in a tattered shawl. Dogar holds up the figure, who looks at the ground with such an intense focus that Ramey cannot see the face.

"Ramey, please," Dogar says, jarring Ramey's trance-like expression. He gestures to help him support the woman on her other side.

"Oh, yes," Ramey says as he steps forward. He can feel the bones in her shoulder. As they walk through the streets, choosing smaller alleys and backroads, Dogar tries to address the woman, but all Ramey hears are muffled moans. He can see she is thin and needs to be supported on both sides. Dogar could not have brought her back alone. They finally reach the inn where a maid comes to help and takes over from Ramey, who stands in the entryway. When Dogar and the maid get her settled in, Dogar comes back to thank Ramey and ask for his help for the following day. As Ramey leaves, he recognizes the hook-nosed man chatting with the innkeeper, but he is too engrossed in his own thoughts to pay him any attention.

Ramey goes back to his own inn, absent-mindedly walks by the innkeeper, goes to his room and lies on his bed staring at the ceiling. He cannot reconcile what he saw today with the lithe and lively girl he fell in love with. The vision haunts him, and he spends a fitful afternoon and night tossing and turning in bed.

Early in the morning, he packs up his belongings and has something light to eat, even though he is unable to taste the food, and goes to Dogar's inn to await his departure. Dogar and his daughter are ready by mid-morning. The girl has washed up and changed into clean clothes, though she still has a ghostly appearance and distracted manner. She is unsteady on her feet.

"I don't know how to thank you, Ramey," Dogar says.

"Please, Dogar, let us not talk about it anymore. Are you ready to head out?"

"Yes," says Dogar, and the three of them make their way to the port. The girl needs to be helped, but she is a tiny bit better than the day before.

On the first day of their voyage, she appears uncertain of her surroundings. A couple of times she is frightened and lets out a muffled scream. Dogar sits holding her hand and whispering to her in a soothing tone. He asks Ramey to sit by her on the other side, which creates a strange sensation for Ramey. He has been close to her body before, but this time he cannot sense the mind or spirit or soul which had so attracted him. Zara or whoever this usurper of her body is, has a physical presence and faint resemblance to the person Ramey knew three years ago. He can see glimmers of familiar gestures and facial expressions. At one point, she looks quizzically at him as if wondering who he is, but then loses the thread of her thoughts. She smiles at Ramey and points to her clothes, as if asking, "Do you want me to take these off?" He turns away and can barely control his tears of rage.

With each day of their voyage her alertness sharpens, and she gains an awareness of her surroundings. "Excuse me sir, weren't you here yesterday?"

He does not know whether to be glad they have rescued her or sad about the condition of the girl who was once so dear to him. He looks her in the eyes, but sees no hint of recognition, only curiosity along with her question.

"Yes, I was here."

"It is a hot day."

"Yes," he replies, "we are traveling along a desert here."

She looks toward the shore. "Is that the desert?"

They get off at the mouth of the mighty Indus to rest overnight. Apparently, she sleeps for nearly the entire day and night as Ramey does not see her. The trip in the smaller boat up the river begins. With each hour they get further away from the oppressive humidity and desert. As more and more trees appear along the banks, salty air is replaced with the breeze from the forest along both banks.

The journey brings gradual but minor improvement in her condition. She speaks more, but only with her father who also appears stronger. When she sees a colorful parrot land on the gunwale of the boat, she tries to catch it. As the parrot flies away, Zara nearly falls into Ramey's lap. She quickly draws back with suppressed laughter—laughing at her own embarrassment as much as at the parrot's agility. A surge of joy in Ramey's heart manifests in a spontaneous smile.

When they finally arrive in Mohenjo-Daro, Dogar and Zara walk away on their own, with words of thanks from Dogar, and a quick glimpse of a shy girl's furtive goodbye. Ramey spends the night at his friend's house, who wants to hear a detailed account of his adventures in the kingdom. Ramey professes genuine exhaustion and sleeps for nearly twenty-four hours before continuing his journey upriver to Harappa.

Zara

CHAPTER 13

Thoughts of Mesopotamia

Back in town for a week, Ramey reports to his cousins on the business side of his trip but says nothing about Zara. He doesn't tell them about the cuneiform script or his desire for the Indus Valley people to learn to write.

He has suffered through years of heartache and mental anguish in trying to forget Zara. He dreams what their life could have been together—but his dreams turn to nightmares when he wakes up. Even in her weakened state, she has pierced his defenses and hurtled him into an emotional struggle that has taken years to escape. Now back in Harappa, visions of the Zara he first met come flooding back. He thinks of the young girl on the cusp of her first bloom when she was too shy to meet his gaze, but images of the wayward creature ready to undress during a boat ride, mingle and overshadow.

It is a constant struggle to take his mind off her. Two of his cousins notice his distracted manner since his return from Sumer. One day in the gem storage room, when Ramey is grading the piles of semi-precious stones and the bags of precious gems, he overhears them talking in the courtyard.

"What do you think is the matter with him?"

"What do you mean?"

"We cooked his favorite dish yesterday—goat meat with zucchini—and he barely touched it. He complained about too much seasoning."

"Maybe he was just not hungry."

"And what about the pink guavas? I sent someone especially to a grove on one of the farms and he barely ate one small one."

"Ramey did not like the strong fragrance—he said they were too ripe."

"They did have a strong scent, but that is when they are the sweetest."

"Nothing is the matter with him. He had a long trip and is still recovering from the fatigue."

"Fatigue? What fatigue? He can lift twice as much as you can and work twice as long as I do."

"I am not talking about his body—it is his mind."

"I don't know what you mean by a fatigued mind. I am going to ask him." And before the other cousin can say anything, he goes looking for Ramey. Not seeing him in any of the obvious places, he calls out, "Ramey, Ramey, are you here?"

Ramey sticks his head out of the storage room, "What?"

This is as far as the cousin has thought and does not know what to say next.

"Oh, nothing. Are you hungry yet?"

Ramey stares at him. "Hungry? No. Why do you ask?"

"Oh. I thought if you were hungry, I could take over whatever you are doing."

Puzzled, Ramey keeps looking at him for a few moments and goes back to work. The other cousin smirks but says nothing.

There was a time when Ramey would have made fun of anyone who spoke to him like this. Now, he merely shrugs it off. Every opportunity he finds, he busies himself with menial, laborious tasks for hours at a time: cleaning the gem-storage area, organizing the stones by size, brilliance, and their market demand, cleaning and sharpening the drills, and all other manner of tedium he can think of. After a few days he has completed many of these chores or they have become so routine they no longer distract him from thoughts of Zara—of the girl from his distant past, his present, and just maybe his future—a thought he is afraid to let in.

He tries to focus on his other passion—to bring writing to the Indus Valley. He has observed first-hand what it has done for Ur, for Sumer, and for Mesopotamia. He is convinced of the goodness of the people of the Indus Valley: their honesty, their clean habits, sense of justice and fair play. He has seen the people of the Kingdom, or the Empire, or whatever they like to call themselves. Many of them are learned, many are rich, and others have great organizational skills. But many more are dirt poor or destitute. Others he met are cruel, or greedy, or out to cheat people. He believes what makes Sumer famous, and the Indus Valley obscure, is not the quality of the people, but because the Indus Valley has no writing or script of its own, and no ability to keep records. If only we could read and write, he thinks, there would be no end to what we could accomplish. His desire to bring writing to the Indus Valley provides him with an alternate focus to the searing memories of Zara.

The first person he thinks of is the potter who already works with clay. He should be sympathetic to a wider use of his materials, as it would bring him greater importance in the community. He picks up the small clay tablet on which the scribe in Ur had recorded his sales, and heads to the potter's work-shop. He has just finished kneading a big vat of wet clay, with a strong odor of wet earth. The smell reminds Ramey of the muddy shoal he had to step into on his journey down the river two months ago. After greetings and some preliminary conversation, he shows the small tablet to the potter.

"What is this, a toy?"

"It is a record."

"A record of what? Are you on the *Panchayat* Town Council now?"

"No, no, the town is safe from me. This is a record of my sales in the Outworld." Ramey looks at the tablet and begins listing the sales: small white beads—twenty, long blue beads—nine . . . quoting from his memory rather than reading from the tablet. The potter turns the small clay tablet in his hand and gives it back to Ramey.

"A record for who then?"

"What?"

"Who is this record for?

"For me?"

"For you? Don't you remember what you sold?"

"I remember it perfectly right now, but what about after one month, or one year, or five years. With this tablet, anyone in my family will be able to read it in ten or twenty years."

The potter has a faraway look on his face.

"You know Ramey, I remember I had some good years and some bad years, but I don't remember exactly which was which. Sometimes my brother and I cannot agree on things we heard from our father."

"If all that was written down, you would not have this problem."

"And we do have plenty of good clay."

Ramey is encouraged.

"But who will write it for me, and how will I learn to read?"

Ramey tells him how writing and reading is practiced in Sumer. Soon it is time for the potter to get back to work and Ramey leaves.

Next, he speaks with one of the weavers, who is busy dyeing a bright tan fabric. Ramey wonders if it is an order from Dogar. When Ramey explains about writing and shows the tablet to him, there is a positive response like the one from the potter. The weaver is eager to keep track of how many bolts of cloth he has woven, and how many yards of fabric he has sold. With fluctuations in the cotton crop, he feels the need to record and preserve such information for himself and for his family.

Ramey walks out of town to a nearby farm of someone he has dealt with. His friend must have begun his day with the first glow of dawn before the sun was up and is about to stop for a mid-morning meal and siesta. The raw smell of freshly tilled earth engulfs Ramey as he approaches the farmer. His friend nods as he eats mouthfuls of corn bread and puréed spinach curry. He periodically takes gulps from a pitcher of yogurt lassi. Ramey's conversation with him is shorter than with the others, but equally encouraging. The farmer trusts Ramey's judgement about the need to record his years of plentiful and poor harvest, even though he is unsure of the details of writing and reading. Ramey feels heartened, even though each of the artisans brings up the difficulty of adopting the literacy practices. They also want to keep all such information private. In the artisan culture of the Indus Valley, everyone treats his methods, techniques, and even quantities of production as a secret. Ramey tells them about the code of secrecy the scribes practice in Ur, and how they take an oath before their gods to be initiated into their profession.

He realizes the adoption of a writing method, as well as a code of secrecy would have to be done by the town council. So, he wants to plead his case and convince them to adopt a system where everyone would learn to read. A few scribes can be taught to write, and the entire Indus Valley would become literate in no time.

Having worked out a plan of action to make the Indus Valley literate and proficient in writing and reading, his thoughts turn to Zara. Is her health improving? Is her body gaining strength? Is she regaining her beauty? And what of her heart? Has she achieved any peace of mind?

There is only one way to find out. He will travel to Mohenjo-Daro and see for himself. He gathers an assortment of beads, necklaces and pendants, and tells his cousins.

"I am going to travel downriver to check the market. The harvest is nearly done in Mohenjo-Daro, so preparations for the harvest festival must be underway. This is the time people want to buy some jewelry."

Ramey has never considered this festival important in the past, but his cousins encourage him to go. Just maybe, travel to Mohenjo-Daro and attendance at the festival will bring him out of his dark thoughts.

The eagerness in his heart with a tinge of suspense makes the journey seem long but effortless. His friend is a little surprised to see him back so soon, but he welcomes him with open arms. Ramey wants to avoid going to Dogar's house, so he roams the marketplace, hoping for a chance encounter. Casual enquiries reveal that Dogar rarely comes out, so there is no choice but to show up at the house, although he is unsure of his reception. The knock on the door is answered by a domestic servant.

"I am here to see Dogar."

The aroma of fresh cooking emanates from the servant's clothes. He must have been in the kitchen preparing a meal and did not like being interrupted.

"My master is occupied. He cannot see anyone."

"He might make an exception for me. Tell him Ramey is here."

"Ramey or no Ramey, Master Dogar has not seen anyone since he returned."

The domestic is about to close the door when Ramey offers him a handful of *cowrie shells* and insists. "Please go and tell him my name—Ramey."

The domestic does not look convinced, but pockets the *cowrie shells* and goes in, leaving the door ajar. Ramey notices how much more seasoning is used for cooking in this town compared to up north. Coming from Harappa, the presence of a servant is also unfamiliar to him. He hears a muffled exchange of words but cannot make anything out. He can only hear doors opening and closing and distant conversation.

Finally, the servant returns with a resigned look. He motions Ramey to follow him with a now smug expression on his face, as if he has arranged the audience as a favor to Ramey. He is taken to an outer room and told to wait. With Dogar's recent reclusiveness, this room must have been closed for some time. Ramey senses a mild fragrance, realizing the servant has sprinkled rose water as an air freshener. Soon he is greeted warmly by Dogar, who looks gaunt but calm.

"Welcome. Welcome."

They both sit down. Dogar faces Ramey and begins thanking him. Ramey holds up his hand and stops Dogar in mid-sentence "Please, don't mention it. Just tell me how she is."

With a somber expression, Dogar gestures with his hands to indicate an uncertain situation. "She is better, but barely so. It is two steps forward and one step back. Her body is slowly recovering, but her mind and heart are in a struggle to break free of the trauma she has suffered."

"May I see her?" Ramey asks. He wants to decide for himself.

Dogar's face reveals a conflict. "Are you sure you want to see her? Remember, she is not the young, bright, beautiful girl you once knew."

"I understand."

Dogar gets up with an uncertain look. He returns a few minutes later holding Zara's hand. Ramey knows it is Zara only because he has seen her in Sumer. The three of them sit down, not saying anything to each other. Ramey steals a couple of glances at her and Dogar stares at the walls, but she keeps her eyes focused on the floor.

"Do you know me?" Ramey asks.

The question hovers in the air without any response.

Finally, Dogar says, "Zara, he asked you a question."

"I know."

"Do you know him?"

"I don't want to answer," she says, not looking up from the floor.

Ramey and Dogar glance at each other, puzzled. Dogar gestures with his hands to display his ignorance. An uncontrollable feeling comes over Ramey and he wonders what set it off. He thought he was in control of himself but now he must use all his will power to stop himself from crying or screaming and bolting out of the room. He summons all his mental strength to control his actions and at least appear calm, trying to analyze the situation. He takes a deep breath and then it dawns on him—it is the mixture of rose fragrance blended with her physical presence. When Dogar asks her about Ramey, beads of perspiration appear on her face. This was the exact combination of two scents in the air when he first spoke with her three years ago at the Spring Dance. She was perspiring profusely from her performance and rose water had been liberally sprinkled on the dancers to keep things cool. He is still overcome with emotions, but at least he knows there is an external trigger—he is not simply losing his mind.

They sit like this for some time and then Zara gets up. "I am tired," she says and starts to walk out of the room. Dogar also gets up and holds her hand. As they exit, Dogar waves goodbye to Ramey who stays seated, absorbed in his own thoughts. Finally, he too gets up and leaves.

Ramey spends the rest of the week at the Harvest Festival and makes a reasonable number of sales, a few of them in the expensive gem categories. Apparently, the Goddess has been good to the people of this town. He keeps struggling with his thoughts and feelings of Zara. Does he feel attraction, revulsion, or any reaction at all? Does she even know who he is or care? He needs time to sort these things out. Although the festival is over, he remains in town, wondering if he should go and see her again. By the third week of his stay, he feels the urgency of returning to Harappa, so he decides to see Dogar again.

This time the servant does not hesitate and leads Ramey to the sitting room. Ramey hears a muffled conversation but cannot decipher anything.

"Greetings, Ramey. Blessings of the Goddess be upon you," Dogar says as he enters, with Zara in tow. She tilts her head at an angle. As she raises her left eyebrow, a faint smile touches her lips. Ramey sees a shadow of that arch look of hers from many years ago. Her smile and her expression disappear, but she is not as reticent as the last time.

"Greetings," Ramey says to Dogar as he looks again at Zara. There is a faint hint of color in her checks, and she appears to be more alert.

"How have you been?"

She speaks as if she has just been awakened. "Me? Oh, yes, I am here."

This time she holds her gaze on Ramey, as if searching her memory, and then turns to Dogar and whispers, though Ramey can make it out.

"Father, I think I should know this man, but I am not sure."

Dogar smiles in affirmation. Ramey spends more time but there is not much conversation. Finally, as he gets up to leave, she stares at him with a quizzical expression.

Ramey suffers through the upriver trip again, although his heart is more at ease. He has been gone nearly a month, and the following Thursday is the day on which the five men who are the governing committee for Harappa will assemble in the late afternoon. If there are significant matters to discuss, or petitions to listen to, their session may continue into the early evening. Otherwise, the council members will discuss the weekly goings-on in town, exchange social pleasantries, greet any residents who stop by with news of the week, talk to some of them who have been to other towns or into the countryside, and adjourn. Ramey believes it is his duty to visit the five after his trip to pay his respects, respond to anything they might want to know, and then see if the gathering is conducive to a discussion of writing and tablets. He goes back to his family compound to sit down with any of the cousins who are not busy.

"I'll be visiting the council meeting on Thursday afternoon, to talk to them about adopting a script," Ramey tells them and leaves.

One of the cousins turns to his brother. "He is really going to see the Council?"

"That is what he said."

"Well, he seems calmer after his trip to Mohenjo-Daro."

"This writing project may bring him out of his distraction—whatever the cause."

"Let us hope so. I never thought he would be so preoccupied with anything."

They shake their heads and wander off to perform their afternoon chores.

CHAPTER 14

Indus Valley Script

The council members do not seem convinced they need a report from Ramey, but decide to give him a brief opportunity before they get down to the serious matters. The monsoon is late this year and there is still a lot of dust in the air. Before the council meeting begins, a man with a goat-skin water bag flung on his back sprays water on the ground in the assembly area. The water dries very fast, but the fragrance of newly sprinkled damp earth rises and lingers over the assembly, providing a measure of welcome coolness.

The aroma triggers a strange and unexpected feeling in Ramey, and he once again struggles to keep his focus on the here and now. A painful memory of fleeting happiness and devastating sadness engulfs him. When the council meeting starts, he shakes his head, clenches his teeth and tries to pay attention.

"Young Ramey, it is good to see you back safe and healthy. What is it you want to present to us?"

The headman speaks with a distinct tremor in his voice, accompanied by slight wheezing, a testament to his advanced age.

Ramey attempts to control his thoughts. "I have been to Sumer, the kingdom of the two rivers, and I saw how they record all important matters. After my trades I went to a scribe, and he prepared these records for me." He passes the small clay tablet around. "It tells anyone what I sold."

"It does not tell me anything," says one of the councilmen.

"Sorry, councilman. I should have said, for anyone who knows how to read, which most people in Sumer do. If we could also read in Harappa, it would tell us too."

The council member in the fabric business scratches his chin. "So, with writing, I could know what my uncle sold when I was young, and my young son would know one day how many bolts of cloth I wove this year?"

"Yes," Ramey says, "exactly. I suggest the council consider this."

Ramey sees two skeptical faces in the five-man council and notices a man whispering to them from behind. This stranger is not from the Indus Valley but is oddly familiar to Ramey.

"How often do we get the floods?" Ramey says. "What ceremonies do we perform on holy days? All that can be recorded and kept for generations to come. Even details of the harvest—when were the good years and when were the bad. If we start writing, we could know about my grandfather's life and his father's life."

The old headman looks pensive, perhaps contemplating his own mortality and wishing he could leave a record of his life for his son and grandson. At least three of the five members look convinced and willing to consider what he is talking about.

Ramey summons his courage. One of the members who originates from the pottery clan, holds out his hand and Ramey gives him the tablet. The potter feels its heft, turns it around and feels the texture of the inscription.

"You made these marks?"

Obviously, he has not been listening. Ramey shakes his head,

"No, council member, a scribe did. When I went to him, he took a pat of moist clay, flattened it, then made the marks as I told him my sale. Then I took the damp tablet to another man who fired it." The potter runs his fingers over the inscription again, then holds the tablet up at eye level to gauge the sheen on its surface.

"Not bad firing. How big was the kiln?"

"I think small, council member." He indicates the width by holding up his two hands a little under one yard apart, knowing that the potter's clan uses very large kilns that take days to operate for each load.

"How did he fire it? With coal?"

Ramey shakes his head, "I don't know, council member. I left this one day and got it back the next day."

It is better not to go into the details of the firing process as the potter knows it in much better detail. There being no further questions from the council members, Ramey steps back, giving others in the assembly the opportunity to ask questions or express their opinions.

One of the men holds the cuneiform tablet in his hand. "Is this the seal of the man you call skreeb?"

"Scribe," another man corrects the speaker.

"No neighbor, this is not a seal," Ramey says, "It is a record of my sale."

The man thinks for a while. "We all have our unique family seals. I think we should add some symbols saying the name of the family."

There are approving looks all around. One of the men proposes it to a council member, who tentatively agrees. This may be something that can be adopted right away."

"How do you know all that from this shard of pottery?" asks a man in the crowd. Subdued laughter breaks out.

A couple of people who have heard the explanation from Ramey give disapproving looks. Ramey swallows, and smiles from a corner of his mouth. "Yes, neighbor, it is a mere shard of pottery. But when it was wet clay, these marks were made with a stylus pen made of sharpened reed. These symbols have sounds for words."

The wisecracker in the back speaks up again, "What sounds and words can be on this piece of pottery? It cannot speak."

This gives Ramey the exact segue he needs. "Long blue beads—nine, round grey beads—twenty, and so on." He waits to see the response, then continues. "This could be the names of my father's father's father, and all his sons. This might be the contract for the sale of twenty bales of cotton or for dividing the fields between cousins. Anything. Even prayers to the Goddess can be written and put in the house for blessing."

One of the council members who has been quietly following this back and forth in the audience, speaks up. "What young Ramey is saying is that Harappa can be a place where we all write and read, like in Sumer, so we can keep our own records."

"The pottery speaks to young Ramey but does not speak to me," the wisecracker says.

"Yes, neighbor," Ramey smiles, "We all have to learn to read and write in the same way or else it means nothing."

One of the jewelers stands up. "We want to write and record to know how much we sold five years before, and ten years before, and who my father's father's father was, and how many years he lived. We want to know all these things and bless our houses with prayers to the Goddess, so we want to learn writing." He looks around, acknowledges several approving looks, and sits down.

"Fine," the headman says, "The council will consider young Ramey's proposal and make a determination in one month."

It perplexes Ramey why such an obvious need as writing cannot be agreed upon immediately, but he will be patient and wait for the council's decision. On his way home he walks by a small rose garden. Deep in thought about how the Indus Valley will change if writing is adopted, the fragrance of roses once again distracts him. He wants to go back to Mohenjo-Daro. He tells himself he is interested in learning about the business Dogar is in—ores and metals—trades and skills that are far more advanced in Mohenjo-Daro than in Harappa. But of course, he wants to see Zara. He struggles to define his feelings towards her. It may not be the passionate love he felt years back—perhaps that flame has been extinguished. Is it mere sympathy or even pity? All he knows is he must see her.

One week later he is with Zara. Dogar feels comfortable enough leaving the two of them alone, so he leaves the house to take care of some matters in the market. Her strength is beginning to return and she even talks to Ramey, although he is still not sure whether she recognizes him from her past or not.

"So, you make and sell jewelry?" she asks.

"Yes, I brought a necklace for you." Ramey takes out a glittery gem necklace. She looks at it, then at him, but does not touch the necklace as if unsure what he wants her to do with it. Once or twice, she raises her hand but that is all.

"It is for you." He holds the necklace out towards her. She shrinks back, visibly alarmed.

"I know what it means. I don't want it."

Ramey is confused. He has not meant to upset her. It dawns on him that any jewelry or money she was given in Ur led to liaisons of the kind she does not want anything to do with now. He withdraws the necklace and puts it aside.

"I will keep it. You can ask your father about it when he comes back."

No longer alarmed, she is now at ease with him.

To change the subject, he shows her the clay tablet from Ur. "Do you know what this is?"

She laughs, not the carefree laughter he remembers from the old days. She does not feel confident expressing any emotion, not even joy.

"Of course, I know. It is a clay tablet."

Ramey hands it to her. She touches it tentatively and immediately puts it down.

"Do you know what it says?"

She has not expected the question so now focuses her attention and begins to read.

"Long, blue ..." she stops, looks up at Ramey with a sheepish look. "I cannot read very well."

He understands. "I presented it to the council, and I am baffled they did not immediately adopt it."

"Perhaps they need time to talk to each other."

"But Zara, who would not want to write?"

He thinks she should be sympathetic to his ideas about writing in the Indus Valley—after all, she has seen its value in Sumer. She looks at him with wide open eyes.

"Why do you care if Indus people can write or not?"

His passion for writing heats up. "I care so we can become better."

She laughs at his concerned face, reaches over and touches his hand lightly, but immediately draws back, as if she has crossed a line. "This writing idea has made you worried."

He sighs, "All right, then Indus will remain illiterate."

She gives him a gentle push as if to dismiss his problem. In an exaggerated, mock gesture, he falls to the floor. She is alarmed but then realizes the joke and laughs—and he laughs with her. Ramey's feelings confuse him. Is this show of intimacy born of his recent time with her, or is it a rekindling of an old ember left under the ashes of her years in Sumer?

Sitting on the floor, the face of the stranger he noticed at the *Panchayat* Council meeting flashes before his eyes. "I must investigate this," he thinks and climbs back onto his seat.

CHAPTER 15

Dancing Girl in Bronze

The next day Ramey takes the boat back home. Without mentioning Zara to anyone, he tries to catch up on his chores. He is still puzzled about the man who was whispering to the two dissenting council members. Why would this stranger be trying to keep the Indus Valley illiterate? A couple of days later while he is sorting out the storeroom, it finally hits him. The stranger is Arkan, the hook-nosed man he saw in Ur in the alley of the scribes and other random places. What is he doing here? Ramey recalls clearly now the king's spy had lingered in the alley and gone to speak with the scribe after Ramey left. He must have discovered that Ramey was trying to learn to read and write in the cuneiform script of Mesopotamia.

This spy has followed Ramey to Harappa making it his mission to hinder the progress of the Indus Valley civilization. If the Indus people are not going to teach the Sumerians their jewelry making technology, they should not be allowed to take anything from Sumer. Arkan believes Ramey is trying to steal their writing methods and if allowed to start writing and recording, the community-based Indus Valley will become a rival to the monarchy of Mesopotamia.

The following Thursday, Ramey attends the council meeting to hear the council's decision about adopting writing and reading in the cuneiform script. Unless all five council members agree, nothing can be implemented. The headman speaks first, "The council has considered young Ramey's proposal for us to adopt writing, like they do in the kingdom of two rivers. Three of our council members agree, but two are opposed. The council has decided to try writing by adding the family name to each seal using a new script system. If it is found useful, we will consider expanding it after five years."

One of the dissenting council members apparently claimed it would be a waste of time. "Our artisans should be weaving cloth, or making pottery, rather than scribbling symbols." Ramey almost wishes they had a monarchy in the Valley so the king could order the town to adopt writing and for everyone to start writing in the same script. Disappointed and frustrated, he can see the workings of the hooked-nose man in the denial of his proposal.

Ramey remains resolute—he will not give up. He wants to bring writing to the Indus Valley and does not want to wait for five years. He has seen the value of writing in Sumer, and he wants his native place to have the same advantage. If the council does not want to order the townspeople to do it, he will go from house to house and convince the residents. It may take him a year or two, but he is sure they will understand, and he will succeed.

That evening when returning home late from dinner with friends, he notices the shadow of a man following him. When he slows down, the shadow also lingers. When he speeds up, it accelerates. At first, he is spooked but after a while decides to confront the man. He turns around and walks towards him. The shadowy figure turns abruptly and walks away from him. As if not familiar with the street layout, the man enters a blind alley. Ramey soon catches up while the figure tries to meld into a dark corner.

"Who are you and what do you want?" Ramey asks calmly, standing a few paces away.

When there is no answer, he repeats his challenge more forcefully.

"Mind your own business," the man whispers in a heavy accent Ramey recognizes from Sumer.

"I am minding my own business," Ramey says.

"No, you are interfering with the empire. Hiding things from us—trying to steal our achievements. We don't like that."

"I don't care whether you like it or not. I want the Indus Valley to benefit from progress—now."

"You will regret this."

"What can you do to me?"

"Maybe we cannot harm you, but we can harm someone near you."

Ramey hesitates. Is this man threatening his mother, his cousins? He can protect them.

"What will you do?"

"We will reveal personal details. We will tell everyone. She will be disgraced."

Ramey realizes he is threatening Zara who is in a precarious physical and mental state. His heart sinks. Her anonymity in Mohenjo-Daro is her only shield. She grew up in Harappa, four hundred miles upriver and has no friends or acquaintances in this town. Any adverse publicity or other action taken against her would push her over the precipice to a complete mental breakdown, perhaps even to madness. Nothing is worth that risk. Not even the literacy of the Indus Valley. The cuneiform script must eventually reach here but it can be postponed. Zara is dearer to him than his literacy mission. He lost Zara once before. He will not take a chance now.

"Leave her alone."

"We will leave her alone if you abandon your efforts."

The Indus Valley will have other opportunities, but Zara won't. "I promise," he says.

"What did you say. I can't hear you?"

Ramey takes a deep breath and the Zara of his dreams appears. He can almost touch her. The cuneiform letters in the distance fade away.

"What did you say?" the man insists.

Alone with his thoughts of Zara, Ramey gathers his courage. "Can't you hear me? I said I am giving it up. You can keep your precious cuneiform and your empire and everything that goes with it. You have already hurt her enough. Stay away from her."

Ramey quickly turns. With a heavy heart he walks back home. Over the next few days, he tries to focus on his work but cannot. Some of the people who initially heard him preaching about writing and reading try to remind him, but he pretends to be too busy. There is only one avenue to ease his mind and follow his heart.

Ramey tells his cousins he is moving to Mohenjo-Daro. "The market for our exquisite jewelry creations is much better there."

They have seen the money he made during his last stay and are happy for him to continue with his venture. When he is in town, he is in a morose state and simply buries himself in his work. This is the first time he has expressed a desire to undertake something new, so even his mother accepts his forthcoming absence.

Of course, it involves another boat trip, but he does not mind. Every stroke of the oars brings him closer to Zara. When he arrives at Dogar's house, he is shown inside. Soon Zara enters the room, pleased to see him.

"I was thinking about you," she says holding her hands together nervously.

"Me too," he says, not sure about her state of mind or whether she really recognizes him from years ago. But he is content to sit with her and chat, or simply look at her. A little more vigor has returned to her body and mind since he saw her last, but he does not want to test her limits.

"Did you notice I have a new shawl?" she says shyly, caressing the red shawl in her lap. This is the shawl from the fast-talking salesman in Sumer. Ramey left it at Dogar's house hoping Zara would find it. Seeing her caressing the red woolen fabric brings tears to his eyes. He has fulfilled his promise to the Zara he used to know. Somewhere deep down that girl must still be inside this Zara sitting beside him.

"Yes, it is very attractive." He is casually open with her but careful not to cross the boundary into intimacy. After nearly an hour of chatting, she appears tired, so Ramey leaves.

He stays in town and rents a house so he can set up an outpost for his jewelry work—or at least that is what he tells his family. Settling into the new house keeps him busy for the whole week, but then he can't resist going to her house again. Their meetings become more frequent and soon they discuss almost everything—except their feelings. He is content to go on like this while still devoting himself to the business of jewelry selling on the other days. With his continuous presence in town, his family's original products, and the town's obsession with glittery objects, he soon establishes himself as a superior jeweler offering distinctive items. His high-quality gems appeal to the status conscious residents of Mohenjo-Daro. Gradually he increases the time he spends with Zara. Days, weeks and a few months go by, when he senses her developing an affection for him. But if she connects him with the Ramey she once knew, she never lets him know. And he never asks.

Dogar, now accustomed to leaving them alone, allows Ramey free access to the house. Dogar believes the contact with Ramey is good for Zara. If he feels even a tinge of guilt for keeping them apart, he never expresses it. He accepts the current bond that exists between Ramey and his daughter and like Zara, he never refers to their past relationship,

One day as Ramey gets up to leave Zara, Dogar is also leaving home.

"Where to?" Ramey says.

"I am going to check things in my metal workshop."

"I have been meaning to ask," Ramey says, "where exactly is your workshop? I was expecting the hearth to be inside the house."

Dogar laughs, "Yes, I do have a small one inside the house for final processing, but melting copper and tin requires a lot of heat and creates too much smoke and fire. The house would be filled with fumes."

"I understand," Ramey says, "may I come with you."

"By all means. Let us turn right here."

Dogar's metallurgy workshop is situated at a propitious location, taking full advantage of the hilly topography of Mohenjo-Daro. A small hill hides it from the residential area, so the smelting of metals can be done unhindered without drawing complaints from the townspeople. Three workers are stoking the fire under a clay hearth, using a combination of wood, coal and sulphur. The work requires only one man, but the three take turns getting close to the fire and keeping it alive. Ramey approaches the work area and then quickly steps back. It is very hot. The copper ore is piled on the ground to one side and the fuel on the other.

"Where do you get this from?" Ramey asks, pointing to the pile of mixed rock and copper.

"From the western hills, as I told you before."

Ramey sticks around watching the whole operation. He wants to see the final steps.

"And what do you do with it?" he asks, pointing to the melting copper.

"Much of it we cool into ingots that are carried to Mesopotamia where they have an insatiable demand for the metal. The rest we shape into tools, although that requires an additional step of adding tin to copper to make it into bronze."

"Tin? Another metal, so more heat and more melting. Why go through all that? Why not use copper?"

Dogar smiles, "Not so simple, but not very hard either."

"What do you mean?'"

"It requires 1200 degrees to heat pure copper and it is too soft. Adding tin makes it much harder and turns it into bronze, so tools can keep their shape and their sharpness. Tin melts with only 400 degrees of heat, so we don't need separate fires."

"Tools? What kind of tools do you make?"

"Axes, hammers, knives—you name it, and we make it."

"So, you can mold it into any shape?"

"Almost. Last month we had a request for twenty javelin points from some hunters."

Ramey's eyes brighten. Now here is an opportunity that requires an artisan's skill. All that heating and melting and ingot-making may be hard work but does not require an artisan's skill. Molding molten metal into javelin points and tools is akin to jewelry making, obtaining a resource from the earth and shaping it into something useful. Perhaps it can also be shaped into things that are beautiful and artistic, like a piece of jewelry.

From that day on, Ramey dedicates himself to working on and learning all about copper and bronze —especially bronze—the material hard enough for precise shapes. Dogar can find plenty of help for crushing the ore, separating rock from copper, and for heating and melting. But shaping it, especially for bronze tools, requires dedication and skill, which many manual laborers either do not possess, and are unwilling or incapable of learning. Ramey with his jeweler's skills and an eye for aesthetics, rapidly gains an understanding of the material. With gems and rocks, the delicacy lies in their brittleness—one wrong stroke of the jeweler's hammer and the gem shatters and is rendered useless. With bronze, the urgency is in shaping it before it cools off and becomes too hard.

Ramey can withstand the heat of the furnace while melting copper and the tedium of smoothing and polishing the cast figurines. He has the patience to carve with precision and set the clay or wax molds in which to pour molten copper. What irritates him the most are the fumes and smells from the melting ore, which must be tended continuously to remove the mineral matter and slag. He covers his mouth and nose with a scarf to filter out the air during the smelting operation, but he has no way to protect himself against the eye irritation. The combination of fumes, smells, smoke and acrid vapors makes him realize what Dogar had told him at the outset—a metallurgy hearth cannot be operated in a house—this work must be done in a separate building.

Ramey manages to find free time to be with Zara. She looks forward to seeing him, but there is still a curtain between their feelings he is cautious to draw back, and she is reluctant to even touch it. They are now close friends, but will their relationship ever lead to anything further? Their familiarity grows but at such a slow pace it frustrates Ramey and drives him to bouts of hopelessness. He searches for the Zara he once knew in the Zara he is now seeing but there are only glimpses of his former beloved.

Most people in the Indus Valley keep clay or wood statuettes of the Goddess in their homes to help them focus during their prayers, even though they know she is a supernatural, metaphysical entity. The custom in Sumer is to use metal sculptures, at least in the temples and homes of people who are wealthy. Ramey has seen cheap clay and wood figurines of Sumerian gods being sold at the trinket shops around the temple. He has seen bronze sculptures in the temple and understands those must be cast by true believers and dedicated adherents of the faith under the supervision of priests. Dogar casts small figurines of the Sumerian gods that store owners in Ur sell to rich pilgrims who take them to the temple to be blessed by a priest for an appropriate donation. Ramey helps in casting a few of these and his skills sharpen.

As Ramey gains more knowledge in casting bronze figurines, he decides to create his own Zara in bronze—the way he remembers her from the Spring Dance many years ago—vibrant, confident and enticing. He will cast a statue as he desires her to be, not limited by physical reality. The bronze Zara will come from his heart and dreams and not from his head. He decides to make her even younger than when they first met. The bronze Zara will wear the bangles she wore at the Spring Dance—twenty-four on her left arm and four on her right—but this time the bracelets will be his design and creation—something he has never been able to do for her and she is too cautious to accept. The bronze Zara will even wear one of his necklaces.

As he visualizes his creation, he recalls sensuous details when he first saw her so many years ago. At the Spring Dance, she was clothed in light cotton fabric. As her performance progressed, she began to perspire profusely. An attendant came by at intervals to sprinkle rose water on the dancers to keep them cool. They also sprinkled rose water on the audience to freshen up the air and drown any odor of sweat. The fragrance of freshly crushed roses is still deeply embedded in Ramey's memory. Towards the end of the performance, Zara danced with such abandon that when the performance ended, she was drenched. Her thin clothing clung to her shapely body. Whatever of her form was not outlined, Ramey's imagination supplied.

This time he will not keep the sensuous details within his imagination, he will express them in bronze. It takes Ramey half a dozen attempts, but he improves in carving the wax mold, pouring the molten bronze, smoothing out the rough edges, and polishing it to a gloss. He tinkers with how much tin to add to get the malleability and ductility just right. Imagining Zara's love of bangles, he covers her left arm with hoops of his own creation. He remembers how she once held her hand out to offer him a sweet as if the hand was beckoning him. So why not a statue also mirroring that gesture?

One day one of Dogar's helpers sees Ramey working on the wax mold. "Which Sumerian god are you casting?"

"Not Sumerian. This one is for Babylon." The answer is sufficient for the helper, allowing Ramey to finish his work. Finally satisfied with the mold and casting, he does a final smoothing and polishing. Rather than showing it to Dogar or any of his helpers, Ramey takes it to the house he is living in and positions it in the center of his altar. A fitting place for *Dancing Girl of the Indus Valley*.

Ramey continues to find plenty of opportunities to spend time with Zara. By the end of the year, she has developed a deep affection for him. They do want to be free and bounteous to each other. And so, a gentle affection leads to a gentle love.

He can no longer hold back and one day he asks her, "Zara, do you think that you can be happy with me?" She looks up at him with moist eyes as Ramey holds her hand, "I do love you—you must know."

Tears begin falling from her eyes.

"Why do you cry? Are you not pleased?"

Her face is stained with tears, but a smile appears on her lips as her right eyebrow arches up.

Inspired by 4,500-year-old bronze figurine, Indus Valley

It is another six months before they marry. It has been a little over four years since the Spring Dance that first brought them together. A few relatives from Harappa make the journey to attend the wedding. He warns them not to mention Harappa, the Spring Festival or *Dancing Girl*. The wedding is a small affair. The only people from Mohenjo-Daro who even know about it are Dogar's workers and Ramey's friend Berum. Along with the guests they are treated to a sumptuous meal with a rare treat of desserts. It is not yet the sugarcane season, so the desserts are made from beets, giving them a distinct syrupy flavor.

After the ceremony Zara moves in with Ramey. In a few days, he notices how she often carries the red shawl with her. It is not particularly cold, but she frequently wraps it around her shoulders. Other times, she folds the shawl next to her. With one hand, she caresses it lightly as if she finds the touch reassuring and comforting—or perhaps even sensuous. He hopes the shawl will help her rediscover distant but pleasant memories buried under her bitter time in Sumer.

A few more days pass before she notices the altar and makes it a regular routine to stand by it to do her devotion. She performs a ritual of sprinkling a few drops of rose water around the altar before she prays. Ramey wonders what she is praying for—or if she is confessing to the Goddess. He has been doing the daily devotion on his own, but her presence combined with the lingering fragrance of freshly sprinkled rose water brings back all his old memories. After performing her devotion and prayers, she stands by the altar examining the figurines. She touches them one by one as if trying to identify who or what they represent. She seems to be familiar with the clay and wood statuettes of the Goddess, and even the metal figurine of a god from Sumer. Even when she is not praying, Ramey finds her standing by the altar a couple of times a day.

One afternoon as she raises her hands to touch one of the figurines, Ramey hears a clinking sound. Startled, he looks around. She is wearing bangles on her left arm—not a lot like the old days, but four or five. This gladdens his heart.

"Who is this figurine in bronze?" she asks.

Ramey sees no hint of recognition in her eyes.

"Oh, let me think. This is a young girl."

"I can see she is a young girl, but who is she? Why is she standing like that?"

"Hmm."

"Don't play games with me, Ramey." Beads of perspiration appear on her forehead and her eyes fill with tears.

"I think she is about to begin a dance."

"But who is she?"

"I call her *Dancing Girl of the Indus Valley*."

Zara flinches and turns away, pretending to busy herself.

After a few days, she brings up the figurine again. This time in a pensive mood.

"Do you know her?"

"Not anymore."

"Is she still alive."

"I hope so, but I don't know."

"Do you love her?"

"I don't love anyone as much as I love you," he says, and he kisses her. She melts into his arms like when they first met and looks at him with loving eyes and a smile. While she holds his gaze, she jingles her arm as if answering all his questions. He understands she knows who he is and who she was—and how they were together.

In that moment, the bronze *Dancing Girl of the Indus Valley* transforms into his beloved Zara. He picks up the figurine and places it on the altar where it belongs. His true Zara is in his arms.

Dancers

Epilogue

Time passes and with its passage so do Zara and Ramey. After several centuries, the Indus Valley civilization also passes into oblivion. And after another millennium, even the great empires of Mesopotamia disappear. In 1926, four thousand and five hundred years later, during the excavation of a pile of rubble called the "Mound of the Dead" or Mohenjo-Daro four men and women archeologists discover a bronze figurine, Dancing Girl of the Indus Valley—the Zara of this story.

Dancing Girl in Bronze

*Bronze figurine excavated during an
archeological dig in Mohenjo-Daro in 1926*

Acknowledgements

My sister Qaisera organized the trip to the ruins of Harappa and accompanied me there. During the night spent in proximity to the remnants of the ancient town, I sensed a myriad of untold stories of long ago people, and grasped onto one of them. This book is an attempt to tell that story.

My daughter AliA spent endless hours drawing and redrawing, trying to interpret my vague descriptions of an unseen ancient people, and turning them into aesthetically pleasing works of art.

Martha Fuller assiduously edited my manuscript, smoothing out kinks and removing barbs and nettles.

Sharon Rawlins expertly turned my text and AliA's paintings into an attractive book.

I am indebted to all of these women.

About the Author

Arshud Mahmood was born in India, grew up in Pakistan, and came to California over 50 years ago. He received a Ph.D. in engineering from the University of California, Berkeley and works as a consulting engineer. The ancient Indus Valley Civilization is an area of personal interest and study for him—harking back to his Punjabi family. His curiosity about this ancient civilization is expressed in his imaginative story—*Dancing Girl of the Indus Valley*. His first short collection, *Coffee with Chicory* (2011) is available on Amazon in print or on Kindle.

About the Illustrator

AliA was born in California, spent her childhood in Texas and Alaska, and currently lives in Southern California. She received a B. A. in Fine Art from Art Center College of Design in Pasadena and works as a freelance artist—creating paintings, drawings, tattoos, and wearable art. (aliatalent@gmail.com)

This book is typeset in Museo, a contemporary semi-serif typeface. Display type is Marydale, a handlettering font. Cover type is Orpheus Pro, a serif typeface.